US AGAINST EVERYBODY: A D̶ ̶ ̶ ̶ ̶

TALE 3   MISS CANDICE

Us Against Everybody 3

A Detroit Love Tale

Miss Candice

Text LEOSULLIVAN to 22828 to join our mailing list!

To submit a manuscript for our review,
email us at leosullivanpresents@gmail.com

Previously

Vice

I didn't give a fuck. Once I made it on the freeway and seen all the cars backed up, I hopped out and ran to the scene. They tried to keep me back, and they did a good job at it. Storm's car sat in the middle of the freeway, smashed up. The cops didn't want to give me any information. Even after I lied and told them pussy niggas the victim was my fiancé. They didn't give a fuck but the people in traffic did. The ones who seen and heard everything. They gave me some valuable information. Sent me right on my fucking way.

Now, I sat in the whip with Dawson, chiefing from a blunt full of the best loud in the city. Of course it was the best; it's my shit. I picked cuz up as soon as I left the scene. I had to. It was only right. Reek was busy on the block, making sure shit moved swiftly.

I took a pull from the blunt, and looked at the fiery red tip as smoke slowly escaped my mouth. Before I picked cuz up, I hit the liquor store. Chugged a whole pint of Ciroc, straight no chase. I was fucked up out here. My diamond. My fucking diamond was gone. All because of a stupid ass fuck nigga.

I pulled off in the direction of the spot on Riopelle, where Reek was working. I couldn't believe a nigga I put on, and looked out for on some one hundred shit was responsible for this shit. I let my conscious cloud my better judgement. Niggas always want the number one spot. Why come for my lil' mama? Brown skin had nothing to do with this shit. I didn't want her involved in this life! Niggas didn't even know about her. Just my two trusted soldiers. Reek and Dawson. Can you believe the audacity?

"Where we going cuz?," asked Dawson looking out of the window.

"Riopelle. Gotta holla at Reek about something."

He looked at me and said, "What it is? You found the black van?"

I chuckled and ignored him as I approached seven mile. He repeated his question and I said nothing. I turned the music up and handed the blunt to him. When he reached for it I looked at his hand, then I jammed the blunt in his eye, and smashed his head against the dashboard.

Never did I suspect my blood. My fucking cousin. The whole mothafuckin time, worried about Reek being a fucking snake. Pulling burners on bro and shit. And for nothing.

While I was standing at the accident scene, begging for information, someone in traffic called me over. I walked up to her car and she told me she heard and seen everything since the accident was literally a few feet away from her. She was behind the black van.

"The young woman was a fighter. I tell you that," she shook her head with tears falling from her eyes, "Two men approached her car after they hit her. As soon as they snatched her door open she yelled 'Dawson! What the fuck!?' She didn't stop screaming his name saying how Vice was going to fuck him up as she kicked and fought trying to get away from them. But the bigger guy, who I'm assuming was Dawson knocked her out cold. He was pissed because the little lady spit in his face and bit him. Right on his hand."

So when Dawson reached for my blunt and I noticed teeth marks in his hand that was all the confirmation I needed. I made a right on Riopelle, just as Dawson was regaining cautiousness. He looked at me with his one good eye, as he screamed at the top of his lungs. I turned the stereo up louder as I parked in front of the spot. Reek came running down immediately. I had already wired bro up with the info.

He hopped in the backseat and I peeled off. Like I said before, I'm not the torturing type. But this shit chea, is the ultimate betrayal.

I turned the music down and calmly told Dawson to shut the fuck up. He didn't. But when I put fire to the blunt and pointed it at him, he did.

"So I'm going to ask you a few questions, *cuz*," I said, adding extra emphasis on cuz.

He cried, "What nigga?! Fuck!"

I laughed, "You mad huh? Keep calm, *fam,* if you make it through this you'll be able to wear a cold ass eye patch." I looked at Reek through the rearview and said, "But we all know this nigga ain't making it, right?"

Reek shook his head and said, "You's a fucking animal, brodie."

"Man what the fuck is this about," yelled Dawson.

I burned him in the face with the blunt and said, "Stop raising yo voice in my fucking car, pussy!"

He squirmed and cried, "What...what's up cuz? We fam—

"You right, we're family! Which is why this shit hurt so bad nigga! Dawg, where my bitch at?!"

Dawson fell silent and looked out the window, his hand covering the other eye. I stomped down on the brakes and pulled the glock from under my seat and pressed it to the back of his head.

"Come on dawg, let a nigga have a little fun for once! I'm not trying to end things this way," I told him.

He kept his eyes on whatever he was looking at outside the window, "I didn't mean for shit to get this bad. You know how I feel about loyalty, man. But I couldn't sit back and wa—

"Nigga, spare me the bullshit. Just tell me where my bitch at."

"You gone let me walk if I do so?"

I smirked and shook my head, "Yeah, cuz, I'ma let you walk."

He tensed up and said, "No the fuc—

I pressed the gun harder against his skull, "Nigga I said I was! You tryna call me a liar?!"

"Aight, aight, cuz! She...she's at Joslyn's spot."

I sat there confused for a minute. Fuck he mean she's at Joslyn's spot. Fuck he mean dawg? Didn't I tell that bitch that if I have any more problems out of her I'm snatching the life right up out of her? I was shocked. So fucking shocked that a nigga was cracking up laughing. There wasn't anything funny though. I was full of rage. So much rage that I pulled the trigger.

Reek yelled, "What the fuck brodie," as he looked around making sure hook wasn't near.

I didn't give a fuck. He realized just how much I didn't care when I pulled off with Dawson's dead body sitting there. Busted window, brain matter, and blood all over my face.

Reek sat behind me and shook my shoulders from the backseat. He was trying to pull me to reality. Trying to tell me I was being stupid sloppy but I didn't care. I pressed my feet down on the gas pedal, heading to Joslyn's spot. Thing is, she stayed down town. And down town is always flooded with hook.

"Vice! Nigga! You gotta pull this bitch over bro! You tryna get us thrown under the jail yo!"

I blinked my eyes repeatedly before finally slowing the car down from seventy, to thirty. I glanced at Dawson and the thought of me having to tell my auntie her son was killed crossed my mind. I felt no remorse from killing him but I did have ill feelings about giving the news to my aunt.

"What we gone do?," I asked as I stared at Reek threw the rearview.

He was silent. Mainly because I've never came at him not knowing what to do. I was lost at the moment. I couldn't think straight and that was because I was imagining what could possibly be going down at Joslyn's spot. How she could be doing my baby was killing me. Brown skin was caught up in all of this shit because of me. I'll never be able to forgive myself if that stupid bitch Joslyn does something like... man I can't even bring myself to say what I'm thinking.

I regretted not offing that emotional bitch when I had the chance. I just didn't think she would be so fucking stupid to do something like this. Now that I think about it, the bitch hit my line earlier. What the fuck could she have possibly wanted? I needed to hurry up and get there before it is too late. I can't even think of how I'd feel if I walked in on some bull shit. In such a short period of time, Storm and I had become one. And if I loss shorty, I'll be losing a piece of me too.

Finally, Reek spoke.

"Pull this bitch in the alley over there," he pointed.

I made a quick left and pulled into the alley, praying to God no one saw us. Dawson's limp body fell against me, and I roughly pushed him off of me. I shifted the car in park and asked Reek what was next.

"Push the nigga out, bro," said Reek.

I looked at him and laughed, "Bet."

I leaned over and opened the door, then pushed Dawson. I didn't even look down at him before I closed the door back and drove away. He was nothing to me. The respect and love I had for him went away once I found out he was behind the shit.

"Swing back around the way. Put this bitch in the garage until we can take it to the chop shop," said Reek, "We can ride in my whip."

I just nodded and kept my eyes on the road. The blood and brain matter was starting to irritate my skin, so I rubbed it away. I placed my hands back on the steering wheel and looked down at the stuff that transferred from my face to my hand. I smirked, fuck nigga. What? Nigga thought he was exempt because we shared the same blood? I told lil' mama! I'll cause havoc out to this bitch. And I meant on anybody!

What had me a little vexed was why? Why did Dawson bitch up and try to play me? I cursed myself for not getting more information before I offed him. But fuck it! Nigga is a goner. That's all that really matters. I couldn't give a fuck less about why.

I drove into the garage at the spot and cut the engine off, before lowering the garage door. I looked in my passenger seat and instantly became pissed. The Audi is my favorite car. Now I'll have to get my baby chopped up. All because a bitch nigga couldn't keep it G!

I hopped out the whip, and Reek did too. He had his phone glued to his ear, talking to the chop shop guy. I started to walk out of the garage, but he held me back. I looked at him like he lost his mind and he motioned at my face. I had Dawson all over me. I yanked away from Reek and stuck my key in the trunk lock. I had all type of shit in here. What was going on had me off my game a lil bit.

I stripped of everything but my draws, and threw the clothes in a little pile in a corner. I grabbed a few wet wipes out of a canister and proceeded to wipe my face and body down. I tossed the wipes in the corner and put a black t-shirt over my head. I slid on a pair of Nike basketball shorts, although it's only about thirty degrees out. That's all I had. I looked down at my shoes and brains were even on them. Fuck! I kicked my Loubti's off and tossed them in the pile, and put on a pair of Gucci flip flops.

I grabbed the can of gasoline out and proceeded to close the trunk. Again, Reek stopped me and shook his head.

When he got off the phone he said, "I know how bad you wanna get to Storm, but we gotta clean the shit up bro."

He looked into the trunk, grabbed some bleach wipes and two rain ponchos.

He handed me a poncho and I put it on over my head. This shit had me so out of my mind, I was about to leave the murder scene dirty. I had to get my head screwed on straight. I grabbed some bleach wipes from Reek and we both walked over to the passenger side, where Dawson took his last breath.

I opened the door and we began to clean everything up. Reek kept trying to make small talk but I wasn't in the mood to rap. All I kept thinking about was getting to my lil' mama pronto. Reek knew I was losing it, so he was doing his best at keeping shit afloat. I appreciated the fuck out of bro for that. He's a trill ass nigga. I low key regret even pulling the burner on him on so many occasions.

After we finished cleaning up, we wiped the car down and got rid of everything I had in it. By time we were finished, the duffle bag I had in the back was full to capacity. I poured gasoline on the clothes, and wipes we used to clean up with and lit a match. Once that burned down to ashes, I swept it up and tossed them in the trashcan.

Finally, we were in Reek's whip, heading to Joslyn's crib. Bro sat there steady trying to talk to me and make light of the situation. He could see the fire in my eyes. He was trying to calm me but it wasn't working. I saw Reek's lips moving but I didn't hear a thing he said.

All I kept thinking of is the last time I held her. The kiss we shared, and how bad I wanted to fuck her. I should've. I wish I fucking would've.

"Her spot right there," I told Reek when we finally made it down town.

My heart raced with fear and excitement all at once.

Reek parked down from her crib and I hopped out before he even came to a complete stop.

Before I made it to Joslyn's crib though, I stopped dead in my tracks. How did I not notice the three squad cars and ambulance parked out front before we parked? My palms began to sweat, and my mouth got dry.

"Fuck, bro," said Reek as paramedics walked out of Joslyn's crib with a body on the stretcher with a sheet thrown over it.

I took off running. A nigga would've thought I ran track if they witnessed how fast I was running. Before I could make it to them, a cop stopped me.

"I'm sorry son, you can't go—

"Who the fuck is that yo? Who's body is...."

My voice trailed off as I witnessed the cops walking someone out of the house handcuffed. I squinted my eyes, trying to get a good look at the person. They were covered in blood. When she walked by me, our eyes met.

I tried to get at her, and she tried to get at me. I tried my best, as did she. We couldn't help it. We were attracting to one another. Like a negative, to a fucking positive. The cop held me back as best as he could, but I eventually got away. But it was too late. Brown skin was already in the back of the squad car. I looked inside at her. She looked back at me. Instead of crying, like she was when they walked her to the car, she was smiling.

What the fuck happened?

1.

STORM

As my nails tapped against the steel table in the interrogation room, I couldn't help but think of the way stabbing into her flesh felt. As traumatized as I was, I played it cool like I was unfazed. But in all actuality, I was losing my mind. As one would expect, I was having a hard time wrapping my mind around the fact that being with Vice was changing me. I've never thought of doing anything as gruesome and unholy in my entire life. But it had to be done. It was either me or her. And anybody with good sense would choose their life over the next. Especially if that bitch was trying to kill you, just like Joslyn was trying to kill me.

How much she tried to explain her reasoning for basically kidnapping me didn't matter. I didn't care about the fact that she wanted to back out. Or how she never really wanted to go through with it in the first place. No, see the point of it all is, she anticipated on killing me. I should've let Vice kill her the first time. Then, I wouldn't be living with the image of her lifeless body lying in a pool of blood as I continued to stab her well after she was long gone. Can't you understand that I was afraid? I wanted her dead. It was either me or her.

If I would've been paying attention, I would've noticed the black conversion van from the night before, trailing me. But nah, I was busy on the phone gossiping with Carla. Even if I wasn't on the phone, I still wouldn't have been paying attention. I didn't grow up having to look over my shoulder. Watching my back was new to me. I wish I would've though. Had I been paying attention I wouldn't have been kidnapped.

Anyway, the black conversion van crashed into the back of my Charger while I sped down the freeway on my way home. My head went crashing against the steering wheel so hard, resulting in a gash. I laid on my steering wheel dazed. My car horn blared as the sound of burning rubber frightened me. I just knew I was going to be hit again. But thankfully, I wasn't. I slowly lifted my throbbing head from the steering wheel. With squinted eyes, I looked at the scene around me. There were car parts everywhere. All from my car. I knew it was totaled.

"Ahh," I cried as I tried to sit up completely straight. My back was in pain as well. I wasn't severely injured but the pain was nearly unbearable.

I sat there for a moment, taking deep breaths. I had to get out and see how the person who hit me was doing. They hit me really hard. See, at first, I thought the accident was my fault. Maybe I was going too slowly? Maybe I wasn't paying attention because I was so engulfed in the conversation Carla and I were having? Those thoughts of guilt were quickly dismissed when my door was yanked open.

It was like the pain I was in was no more, and my survival instincts kicked in. Especially when I recognized my assaulter as Vice's cousin, Dawson. As soon as I turned my head to look at him, I noticed the fire in his eyes. The charm I noticed in them before was gone. If he wouldn't have been so rough with me, I would've mistaken him being there as a rescue. But no, Dawson was rough. He was no longer my boyfriend's cool ass cousin. No, that nigga was the enemy.

Dawson pulled me out of the van and I hit the concrete with a hard crash. I didn't have time to bask in the pain caused by the fall, before he was dragging me. My eyes darted from the left and right, looking for a way out. The people in traffic stayed in their cars, watching everything transpire. They didn't care to help. They knew what was going on. I kept yelling help. No one helped. And when I noticed the black van Dawson was dragging me to, I kicked and screamed at him even more. I kept telling him Vice was going to fuck him up. That I was sure of! I was putting up a good fight before he knocked me unconscious and threw me over his broad shoulders.

*

The strong smell of fumes filled my nose, causing me to wake up. When I opened my eyes, I realized that I was taken. I was in the back of the conversion van, wrists tied and mouth gagged. Then, I figured out why I smelled fumes. The van had been in an accident and these niggas were driving it like everything was okay. It sounded horrible, and reeked of burning oil and antifreeze.

I scanned my surroundings, trying to find something that'd help me out of this situation. There was nothing. There was nothing back there with me. Emptiness.

"What you about to do with the little lady?," I heard a man say.

"Me and Joslyn about to do a number on her," I heard Dawson say.

When he mentioned Joslyn, my ears perked up and I pressed my ear onto the wall of the van that separated the front from the back.

"You sure you can trust that broad?"

"Yeah man, she hate the nigga just as much as I do," Dawson said, "Nigga walk around like he's God. Like

he's untouchable. Got his bitch now, let's see how tough he be now."

I shook my head as tears rolled down my face. I was caught up in this shit because of Vice. Thing is, unlike usual, I wasn't even mad at him. I've accepted the fact that risks came with messing with him. I've accepted the fact that this wasn't a normal relationship. Who I was mad at was Dawson because he was fucking with the wrong bitch. Vice has told me over and over again that he'd cause havoc for me. I could only imagine what type of wrath he was going to release on Dawson when he found out.

Still, I was confused at why Dawson was doing this.

"That nigga is going to go bananas," said the other guy I didn't recognized. I've never saw him until today. "You know how crazy he can get. What the hell you fucking with Vice for anyway?"

Dawson was quiet for a few seconds. I heard a loud slap before he responded, "Stop talking about that nigga like I'm supposed to be worried! You working for me, feigned out ass nigga! I don't give a fuck about how you might feel about the nigga. I own you now! I'm doing it because I'm tired of playing second fiddle! Tired of the nigga talking to me all crazy like! This is all your fault anyway! You chose him over me—

"Because he was a smart kid! You and your brothers were nothing but knucklehead dummies! What the fuck would I put any of you on for?

SMACK!

"Pull this bitch over! Now," yelled Dawson.

"Come on man, I'm just keeping it real!"

"You think I'm fucking around Rico? Huh?"

I heard a lot of scuffling before the car came to a sudden halt, sending my body falling forward. I prayed like hell they didn't know I was awake. I hurried and lied my back against the wall and closed my eyes in case they came to look.

I heard Dawson yelled at Rico about how stupid he was. He was downright insulting the man. He sounded like an old man who was only involved because he had a drug habit Dawson was going to support. Dawson was yelling at him about he should've put him on and how he should be the one respected. He was complaining about being in Vice's shadow. He hated it.

Rico didn't sound afraid as he yelled back at Dawson about being stupid. Told him he knew exactly

23

why he didn't give him the drugs. Said if he didn't know then, he should definitely know now. Rico talked about Vice like he cared for him. He complimented Vice on his wits. Said Dawson would've never prevailed in the drug game as well as Vice was. He told Dawson that Vice was a natural born hustler. He even went as far as saying Dawson would never possess those type of qualities and was only committing a death-wish by crossing the coldblooded killer.

I guess Dawson was tired of being insulted and belittled by the crackhead because what I heard next sent a ringing to my ears. Dawson let off a single gunshot. I wished I could've covered my ears. I heard the car door slam, and then another one open. Dawson was pulling Rico out of the car. He talked shit as he did so.

"Fuck you, old man! You don't know a got damn thing about shit! Look at what happened to you! Crackhead ass nigga. Fuck you, and fuck Vice! I'm going to show niggas not to treat me like nothing. Nigga forever popping off at the mouth. You say Vice smart huh? How smart? I sent the pigs to the house on Riopelle, and he's still trying to figure out who did it. I sent Tank to his crib to split his wig. Nigga still vexed about that. Nigga ain't smart." Dawson snorted and said, "Who the fuck he think he is to make my childhood home into a fucking dope spot?! The nigga is disrespectful! I need him out the way! Tank was too

weak to handle it. Pussy ass nigga! What type of cat ain't hard enough to murk a dude who killed his brother? So fuck it. I gotta handle my own dirty work."

Seconds later, I heard him standing outside of the back of the van. I kept my eyes closed. He opened the door and I heard him throw something back there with me. I silently prayed it wasn't what I thought it was. When he shut the door back, I opened my eyes and discovered it was just that. I wanted to scream. There laid Rico, a few feet away from me, with a huge hole on the side of his head. At that moment, I was thankful for the duct tape over my mouth. Had it not been there Dawson would've heard me scream. I shut my eyes as tightly as possible, hoping to get the image out of my head.

*

After what felt like twenty minutes of driving, the car came to a halt. I sat there praying that whatever Dawson had planned for me was a fail. But in the back of my mind I knew it was over. Thing is, I wouldn't give up. I couldn't. My life was far too precious not to fight for. So that's what I did. As soon as Dawson opened that back door to pull me out, I was fighting again. It didn't last long. He climbed over Rico's dead body, shut the doors and stood over me. He blocked my kicks before he was able to grab my wild legs.

"Calm down bitch! If anybody hears anything I swear to God I'll end your ass right now!"

You think I gave a fuck? Nope, sure in the hell didn't. I figured Dawson didn't really want me dead. Not now at least. Otherwise, why go through the trouble of kidnapping me? They wanted to send a message. So I totally disregarded what the fuck he was rapping about and kept squirming and kicking at him. Finally, he had had enough.

Dawson leaned down and knocked me out cold.

*

Once again, I was awake without notice. I opened my eyes briefly, to take in my surroundings. We were at Joslyn's and she was pacing the floor in a black lace bra and panty set. Her box braids were up in a high ponytail. One look at her and it was very apparent that she was distraught and scared. I hurriedly scanned the room with my eyes. My throat instantly turned dry. There was clear plastic covering the floor. In the middle of the room was a wooden chair with robe draped over the seat. I was laid by the front door. I hurried and closed my eyes once I heard heavy footsteps approaching. Dawson was walking towards me.

I kept them slightly open as best as I could.

He gawked down on me, his eyes roaming my body in disgust.

"Help me put this bitch in the chair," said Dawson looking over at Joslyn.

"Umm...umm... I don't think this is a good idea Dawson. You already know that nigga is going to go bananas when he finds out. Vice don't g—

Dawson moved so suddenly that even I flinched. I silently prayed that no one seen me. It was obvious that they hadn't. Dawson was too focused on the hesitation in Joslyn's voice. She stood there with worry written all over her face. Her eyebrows were knitted together, she chewed on her bottom lip, and she couldn't stay still.

Dawson stood in her face and grabbed her by her shoulders, shaking her.

"Don't do this shit right now, Jos! You can't do this shit to me." Dawson grabbed her by her chin and made her look at him. "We both wanted this shit, baby. Don't back down when shit gets real."

Joslyn turned away and said, "I just don't know Dawson. I mean, he made it very clear to me not to touch her. I just would rather not go aga—

Dawson pushed her away and waved her off before sitting on the couch, "I don't give a fuck about you regretting the shit, bitch you gone do what you promised you would."

She glanced at me and I shut my eyes completely.

"I never promised you anything. You found out about what he did to me and decided to reach out to me," Joslyn yelled at Dawson.

He paid her no mind. Dawson's eyes were on me. He knew I was conscious. Dawson stood up, adjusted his designer jeans and walked my way. Since I knew he knew I was up, I opened my eyes and stared at him. Dawson leaned down and snatched me up by the collar of my shirt when he finally made it over to me. I peeped Joslyn shake her head and walk away to the back of the condo.

Dawson slung me around like a rag doll. He totally disregarded the fact that I was a defenseless woman. He threw me on top of the plastic, a few inches away from the chair. He leaned down and snatched the tape from my mouth.

I giggled and said, "Vice is going to fuck you up, boy."

By then, Joslyn was back in the living room. She yelled, "What?! He knows?"

Again, Dawson waved her off and said to me, "Shut the fuck up lil bitch. The nigga ain't gone ever find out. Stupid nigga ain't gotta clue."

I just nodded, "Untie me, Dawson."

He stared me in the eyes. Dawson studied me. He could tell I wasn't the same fragile, gullible, sweet girl he met. Naw, see, fucking with Vice turned me into the woman I needed to be. I had to toughen up. I had to match Vices gangsta. If I didn't I'd forever be a burden to him. He'd worry about me. You see what happened with the Joslyn situation. If I was the bitch I am now, being jumped would've never happened. I would've been strapped with at least a blade. Swear I would've cut a few bitches up.

He pulled me up and sat me in the chair. Although I was crying, I smiled. I knew this wasn't the end of me. It couldn't be. I knew God had much more planned for me. To be tortured and killed wasn't in the cards for me. Couldn't be.

"Why is she smiling," asked Joslyn as she looked out the window. "I swear that nigga a about to run up in here bu—

"Shut the fuck up, Jos! The nigga ain't about to run through shit!"

Dawson walked away and grabbed Joslyn by the arm. He looked over at me over his shoulder and walked a few feet away. I couldn't hear what was said but I was sure he was telling her to stop being so fucking scared. Her being afraid wasn't helping them at all. If anything, it was weakening them. I didn't mind one bit. I planned on pouncing on that weakness and that's exactly what I did when the opportunity presented itself.

They walked over to me. Joslyn stood in my face, her eyes darted from me to Dawson. He told her to do it and I sat there baffled. Do what? Next thing I know, I was being punched in the face. On contact, my bottom lip split and blood leaked from it. I thought that was it, but Joslyn didn't stop there.

She stood behind me, and yanked my head back by my hair. She glared down at me, staring me in the eyes. What happened to the timid hesitate bitch a minute ago?

Dawson stood next to Joslyn looking down at me. He said to her, "Remember what he did to you, Jos baby. He choose her. He disrespected you. Put a gun in that *tight good pussy of yours and threatened to pull the trigger."*

Joslyn's eyes glossed over and she wrapped rope around my neck and pulled on it, so it'd tighten up. I sat there squirming, struggling to breathe as she choked me. I wanted to grab at the robe but my hands were tied. I couldn't do anything. I felt extremely helpless.

Just as I was on the verge of passing out, she stopped.

Dawson grabbed the back of Joslyn's neck and pulled her into a deep tongue kiss, "That's what the fuck I'm talking about baby."

He smacked her on the ass and his phone rung. He looked at the screen and then at Joslyn and then finally at me. Joslyn asked what was wrong and he said it was Vice. He motioned for Joslyn to grab the duct tape and put it over my mouth. I put up a fight but eventually she got it on there.

"Just act normal," whispered Joslyn before Dawson answered.

"What it is, cuz...Oh, alright bet it the fuck up... swing through then my nigga," said Dawson before the call was ended.

Joslyn bit her nails, "You think he know something?"

"Hell naw, the dummy ain't got a clue," said Dawson before grabbing his jacket. "Let me get back to the crib before this nigga get there. Keep this bitch in order Jos!"

She looked over at me and smiled, "Oh, we're going to have some fun."

They kissed before Dawson left.

Joslyn walked to the window and watched him pull off, when she did she exhaled. She looked at me and shook her head and then walked over. She crossed her arms and stared for a few seconds before ripping the tape off of my face.

"Call him and tell him while you still can bitch," I said.

She yelled, "I've tried that! Duh! I called him earlier and he sent me to voicemail, right after that he added me to the block list! I...I don't want to do this anymore!"

I cursed myself. Earlier, when the bitch called him, I snapped. Vice added her to the block list because of me. Shit, I didn't know she was calling to tell him his cousin was setting him up. I shook my head and looked at the stupid broad pacing the floor, biting on her nails.

"Do you have your phone," she stupidly asked.

"Yeah bitch, I had time to grab my phone before Dawson snatched me up out the whip. Don't be dumb ho."

She marched over to me and pointed her trembling finger in my face, "you need to watch yo fucking mouth. Don't forget who has the upper hand bitch."

I hacked up a glob of spit and spat in her face. Immediately, she backed away and wiped the thick, white mucus off of the bridge of her nose. Her mouth was wide open out of shock. The bitch really couldn't believe I spat in her face. But, instead of coming at me on some animal shit, she stood there and cried. She cursed herself, screaming and shouting about how everything was fumed up. I'm the one who was kidnapped, but she was boohooing and losing her mind like she was the hostage.

Joslyn stood in the window, weeping, and thinking out loud I suppose. Well, that's the way it sounded. She went on and on about how she didn't want to do the shit anymore. She couldn't understand why Vice didn't *pick up earlier. Although she knew he was going to be on some animal shit after she told him. But maybe, just maybe, he would've thanked her for the information.*

Joslyn cursed herself for fucking with Dawson period. If only he wouldn't have caught her at such vulnerable stage in her life none of this would've happened. And then, she turned to me and said, "I was only venting to the nigga. I didn't know he wanted Vice dead too. What the fuck? Their cousins! I was shocked when he said he couldn't stand Vice either. I thought he was going to smack the shit out of me for speaking ill on Vice," she shook her head, "I should've known shit was real when the nigga started running plans down to me. Fuck, Vice did me dirty but I'm loyal to that nigga. Us jumping you wasn't planned."

I heard everything she was rapping about but I didn't give a fuck. The fact still remained, she had me hostage in this bitch and even put hands on me a minute ago. I should've let Vice kill her ass before, otherwise this shit wouldn't even be popping off. Joslyn didn't respect me. He told me murder was the only way to obtain respect. I should've listened. Well, I know now.

"Untie me, Jos."

She looked at me like I was crazy and said, "You must think I'm a fool. Let you go for—

"If you let me go, I'll tell him to let you live."

She stood there thinking a second. And then she rolled her eyes, "What makes you think he'll listen to you?"

I twisted my lips up and said, "Let's not forget I'm the reason you're breathing right now bitch. He loves me."

She sucked her teeth, "Vice don't know how to love anybody, bitch, don't let that game fool you."

If I was insecure about the love he confesses to me on a daily, then maybe that would've bothered me. Joslyn was just a bitter ass ex, mad because the nigga she was with for God knows how long, fell in love with me in such a short period of time. Jealous because to him, she was just a cubic zirconia.

"Maybe you're right. But I am the reason you're alive. I can easily persuade him not to do it again."

I was playing with the bitch. I needed her to untie me. I was having a little luck moving my arms around, but Dawson tied them so tight that I was starting to burn my wrist. The more I tried to push the pain out, the harder it got for me to free myself. I twisted my wrist, trying once more. I pulled as hard as I could, but the shit didn't bulge.

35

"Joslyn, are you going to let me go," I asked, helplessly.

She crossed her arms and bit on her bottom lip before saying, "I have to find a phone."

"Don't be stupid now, Joslyn. Nine times out of ten, Vice went looking for me and found out what happened. The good thing about all of this is the fact that you weren't on the accident scene. No one can place you there. If you just let me go, I won't even mention you, I promise."

She scratched her head and mumbled, "She's right." Then she looked at me, "But bitch, I don't trust you! Hell, if I let you go Vice will be the least of my worries, Dawson will murk my ass. No one will save me from him. You can't do that."

"Who are you more afraid of, ho?"

She bit at her acrylics and said, "Dawson. Any nigga crazy enough to go against Vice is not to be fucked over."

I had enough of this bitch. I had a tantrum. I screamed at the top of my lungs and rocked back and forth. She yelled for me to shut the fuck up as she rushed for the duct tape. I didn't. I kept yelling for help. Kept twisting my wrist, kept rocking back and forth. Until, finally.

Crash!

I fell to the floor, and the chair broke immediately. Joslyn's eyes nearly popped out of socket once she realized what happened. The fall hurt like hell, but there was no time to cry about it like a pussy. My will to life was much greater than some temporary pain. I stood up and ran towards Joslyn who was headed for the kitchen.

"Stay back bitch," yelled Joslyn with a butcher knife pointed towards me.

I held my hands up thinking of my next move. I've never been in a predicament where it was either kill or be killed. Hell, I've never killed or even really contemplated killing ever in my life. But for some reason, as I stood there staring at her with the knife in her hand, a killer instinct kicked in like it was my sixth sense.

Still, although I was willing and ready to take a life if that meant saving my own, I didn't know how to approach the situation. Joslyn, with shaky hands, aimed the knife directly at my midsection. What I realized was that I wasn't going to leave this fight without some type of injury. What I wouldn't allow was her to tie me back up. Nah, I couldn't allow that. I can't sit back and hand my life over to someone else.

As we had our standoff, my eyes darted from hers onto the knife. She was nervous and didn't want to be in this situation possibly just as much as I didn't. But when your life is in danger, you fight. So that's what she was doing, no matter how bad she didn't want to. Joslyn knew that if I got my hands on that knife that'd be the end of her. And that's exactly what happened.

As our eyes were fixated on each other, I grabbed the knife. The blade cut deeply in my skin, but I kept a firm hold onto it. Joslyn was yelling about how she was going to kill me. All that did was add fuel to the fire. I held that knife with more force than I've ever held anything. I had to keep it away from me. We tugged back and forth. The more she pulled, the more I was cut. Tears flooded my eyes and I quickly blinked them away. The pain I was in was like no other. But I had to block it. I had no choice. I couldn't let Joslyn win.

I quickly darted my eyes to our feet. We were about a foot apart. Quickly, I tripped her and she went falling to the ground. She no longer had a grip on the knife, so I quickly turned it around. Joslyn kicked me in the stomach and I went flying back into the refrigerator. As I tried to regain my composure, Joslyn stood up. I watched as she went running back towards the kitchen drawer. I shook blood from my hand and ran toward her.

I plunged the knife in her back just as she was pulling another butcher knife out of the drawer. She fell back against me and I pushed her into the kitchen counter. I was in shock. I was in so much pain. Not to mention, I was angry and scared as hell. I couldn't control the rage inside of me as I continued to plunge the knife inside of her.

"Leave me the fuck alone! I never did anything to you bitches! Why fuck with me, huh!? Why fuck with me?!"

I shouted as I continued to stab her. Once I realized Joslyn's body was limp and motionless I dropped the knife and covered my mouth with my hands. I had killed a woman. Never in my life had I imagined my life would spiral out of control like this.

It was either Joslyn or me. So, I had to right? I couldn't sit there and let shit happen. There's no telling what the fuck Dawson had up his sleeve.

"Storm," called the plain clothed detective sitting across from me.

"What," I snapped. I was sick and tired of being questioned when everyone in the police station knew I was the fucking victim, defending myself.

"So, you were abducted and then taken to Ms. Joslyn Givens house, correct." I nodded and he continued, "And you never met the other assailant?"

I crossed my arms over my chest, and shook my head while staring at my wrapped up hand. Of course I knew the other assailant, his face was etched in my mind. The look he gave me. I was traumatized. But, I didn't tell them about Dawson. Why would I? Vice knew. Which meant, Dawson was dead. So I told them I didn't know the other person, just in case his body was found or something.

Anyway, after I did what I did, I screamed. I let out a high-pitched scream and fell to the floor. Shortly after, there was banging on the door. The neighbors had heard me screaming. Next thing I knew, the door was being kicked down and DPD quickly filled the condo. Once they noticed me lying on the ground covered in both me and Joslyn's blood they hurried to my aid. I lied there, incoherently humming as tears fell from my eyes.

Thinking about everything put a smile on my face. I wanted to run to him so badly. When I saw him standing behind the yellow tape blocking Joslyn's house I wanted nothing more than to be in his arms. I needed Vice to tell me everything was going to be okay. I needed to feel his strong arms wrapped around me. I needed him to kiss me on the forehead and tell me I was alright.

"St—

I interrupted him, "I've already told you the story ten times. Please stop asking me the same questions. Quite frankly, it's really bothering me."

I wanted the detective to stop. Running everything that happened down to you was bad enough. I didn't want to relive those events. I wanted to crawl into bed and pretend none of this ever happened. But I knew that'd never be the case. For as long as I live, I'll be the girl that killed the other girl. I'll be the hostage who stabbed her 'kidnapper' thirty times.

"Excuse me, I know you're not speaking to my client without me detective."

I looked up and Carlyle was entering the interrogation room. He nodded and gave me a reassuring smile. The detective cleared his throat and stood up.

"Ms. Hamilton is suffering from serious injuries. She needs to be taken to emergency immediately." The detective sat his card on the table and said, "We'll be in touch young lady."

I deeply exhaled. Finally, I could breathe. Carlyle noticed I was unmoving and walked over to me. He extended his hand and gave me warm smile. I looked up at him and returned it before grabbing his hand.

As soon as we walked out of the room, I bumped into Mack.

2.

JAI

Tati, Storm's ma, called me not too long ago, explaining what happened to Storm. She barely knew anything but what she did tell me was sis was kidnapped and killed one of the people responsible. Swear, the shit she told me didn't sound like Storm at all. She's not a fucking killer – Vice is.

At first I admired the gangsta influence Vice was putting on her, now I'm not feeling the shit. I called her and he even answered saying that she wasn't feeling too well. Duh nigga, of course not why the fuck you think I'm calling her. He wouldn't even give her the phone. He said because he didn't want her talking about the shit I was calling about anymore. We argued and everything. Who the fuck he think he is? Talking about let him take care of her and get the fuck off the line. That's *my* best friend. She has parents. We can take care of her.

Finally, after realizing he wasn't going to give her the phone, I hung up and decided to fuck with Ryan. I couldn't accept the fact that he wouldn't give me the closure I deserved. I need to know more about this baby. I tapped my stiletto nail against my teeth, wondering if I was going too fucking far. Shit, people make fake Facebook pages all day. But I made two. One to add Ryan with and the other to add his baby mama.

"Fuck it," I said as I sent a friend request to his baby momma using the fake page.

She accepted it almost immediately. I'm guessing the fine ass man in the picture I was using persuaded her. I noticed that Ryan didn't comment on any pictures of the baby who happened to be really cute, unlike his pappy. The little boy was a splitting image of his momma who was almost as bad as me. I got a closer look at the picture of her and recognized her from the picture at Ryan's house. What the fuck?

Immediately, I called him. The phone hung up on me and I remembered he added me to the block list. I went straight to the market and downloaded Magic Jack. Magic Jack gave me a completely different number and I called him again. As expected, he answered.

"Who this?"

"Don't hang up."

He sighed, "What now, Jai? A nigga got enough going on as is."

"Who is the girl in the picture at your place?"

"I told you who she was already."

"She's your baby momma too, isn't she?"

Ryan sighed heavily and said, "You on some lurking shit?"

"Stop beating around the bush and just tell me what's up."

"I don't have a damn baby, aight Jai? The bitch is trying to put him on me for mo—

I sucked my teeth and interrupted him, "Yeah, okay nigga. Sure—

"See!? This is why I didn't tell you early. You're too damn childish, shawty. Don't bother calling me again," said Ryan before hanging up in my face.

He was feeling his damn self! Nigga should be honored to have a bitch of my stature sweating him! I didn't even spazz out though. Instead, I sent him a friend request from the other fake page I made and got ready for my night. I didn't want to do anything but cuddle and console my best friend, but her nigga was holding her hostage. So, I got ready for work and headed to Erotic City.

*

After parking in front of the club I made myself three shots of 1800. I didn't feel like the club tonight. I looked up at the building and sighed. Why am I even still working? I swear I wanted to go back to just gold digging. There is nothing like making your own money but I wanted to sit on my ass and stack chips from old ass men. Percy wasn't as consistent as he was before though. I figured I could possibly find me a sucker in here but I haven't been having much luck. Maybe it was because I wasn't trying as hard as I could. Fucking with Ryan had me comfortable. Now that he's on some other shit, I'm about to get on extra grind mode.

I adjusted my titties, and pulled the sun visor down to make sure my makeup was flawless. My eyes were a little puffy from crying over Storm but I still looked good as fuck. Before hoping out the car, I shot sis a text message to let her know I loved and missed her.

As soon as walked in the club my boss, Gino, stopped me.

TALE 3   MISS CANDICE

"You been drinking?"

I waved him off and proceeded to walk away.

Gino grabbed my arm and said, "I'm not kidding around Jai."

I sighed and said, "Yeah, *boss*, I had a little something. What's the problem? Kelly stands behind that bar drinking all damn night—

"And Kelly was fired earlier today. You will be too, if you keep it up," said Gino before walking away.

Did he really think I gave a fuck about this damn job? I chuckled and switched my ass behind the bar. As usual, I spoke to a few dancers and winked at a couple of potential victims. Gino's little threat did nothing to me. I liked having something to do but trust, a bitch is not worried about being fired. I'm not relying on this damn job to pay the bills. I have racks stacked for that. Hopefully I can find me a sucker to play.

I stood behind the bar, rocking my body to Chris Browns new joint Liquor.

There's something in this liquor girl, I'm looking at your figure woah
I just want to see you strip right now, baby let me help you work it out, oh
Girl you look so good, I just wanna get right to it, oh
I could beat it up like-like a real nigga should, baby when we do it, woah

There's something in this liquor, oh yeah
The air is getting thicker
All I want is you-ou-ou-ou
All I want is you-ou-ou-ou

All I wanna do is drink and fuck, drink, drink and fuck
All I wanna do is drink and fuck, and fuck, and fuck
All I want is you-ou-ou-ou, drink and fuck, drink, drink and fuck
Drink and fuck, and fuck, and fuck

As my hips swayed left and right, I looked over my shoulder. I caught him staring at me, but he didn't shy away. He kept his round brown eyes on me. I winked and continued to dance as I grabbed shot glasses from the bottom shelf.

"Excuse me, miss."

I stood up and turned around to face him. I smiled and said, "Can I help you with something?"

TALE 3   MISS CANDICE

He rested his elbows on the bar and smiled at me. His luscious full lips curled up into a smile, exposing a small gap in between his two front teeth. I found it sexy. Everything about him was sexy. I rested my elbows on the bar, staring into his face. Light brown skin, with a head full of waves. Thick nose, with a stubble of hair placed perfectly under it. Strong jawline, with long sideburns connecting to his short beard. He was sexy. Different. I eyed his attire and off bat I knew he had money. On his feet were a pair of Air Jordan's. He wore an iced out Jesus piece, and a seven thousand dollar, diamond bezel Rolex. My eyes went straight to his ring finger, where an iced out ring sat. Although it was covered in diamonds, I couldn't tell if it was a wedding band or not.

"Yes. You can help me with a lot of things," he said before finally sitting on the barstool. "But for starters, what's your name?"

"Jai."

"Nice to meet you Jai, I'm Tech," he told me with his big hand extended.

I shook it and said, "Nice to meet you Tech."

He smiled, "Now, I'd like a shot of Patron." He winked and said, "Maybe you should pour yourself one too."

I poured his shot and said, "I'm good."

I slid the shot to him and he threw it back before saying, "You're going to need it."

I giggled, "Boy, what? Why?"

His once friendly face turned cold, "Vice. Bring him to me. Or…" he gave his North Face coat a pat, "The bullets in my burner will be for you instead of that weak ass nigga."

I nervously grabbed a wash towel, and cleaned the already spotless bar, "I don't know a Vice."

He smiled and said, "Don't lie to me, Jai."

I ignored him and said, "Where you from? I've never seen you around here. You from the west side or something?"

His jaw clinched as he grabbed my wrist, I looked over at security and he turned his nose up and turned away. What the hell? Whoever this nigga is, is definitely about 'that life'. Tech didn't strike me as anything less than a goon.

"Okay, okay! Stop," I said to him as I gave him sad eyes. He released me and I told him, "Vice is too smart for that. I'll help you but you can't use me because he'll know," I looked around the club, "Use one of these random bitches."

"And why shouldn't I go with my first plan? Why in the fuck should I trust you?"

I rolled my eyes and said, "Because he's not going to go for anything concerning me. Vice don't give a fuck about me. Trust! I was trying to get with the nigga for years and he paid me no mind." I smiled mischievously, "Plus, I know the nigga's type."

I scanned the club with my eyes until I spotted Kitten in the back of the club giving a lap dance. She's Vice's type to the tee. Brown skin, petite, with a phat ass booty. But now that I think about it...

"Scratch that shit period," I leaned on the counter, "Vice ain't phasing nobody right now. But his right hand man...Reek...the nigga is a hound. You wanna get Vice, you have to go through Reek."

I scanned the club again, trying to find Reek's type. Which was me. On many occasions, Reek tried to holla at me but I curved the fuck out of him. Mainly because I wanted Vice. But anyway, the nigga like light skin broads with nice bodies. My eyes landed on Bunz who was twerking her big ridiculous Nicki Minaj shaped ass on some scrawny white guy.

I looked at Tech and said, "Bunz. Get that bitch to set them up. I know just the way."

Tech rubbed his chin, "Fuck got you so amped all of a sudden? At first you didn't know the nigga, now you giving me tips and shit."

I shrugged, "My life is far more important than his. The fuck I look like choosing another life over mine?" I poured Tech another shot of Patron, "Gone over there and rap to Bunz. The bitch is a straight up cheese chaser. You're a baller, all you gotta do is floss yo jewels."

Tech stood up and smiled, "Like I did you, huh?"

I rolled my eyes and turned around to put the money he slid over to me in the cash register. I felt shitty for doing what I was doing but like I said, my life is way more important.

3.

VICE

As I stared down at the stack of papers Carlyle laced me with I was in disbelief. It had been Dawson the entire time. Dawson was a fucking informant. He was helping the pigs hit my spots. I couldn't believe my fucking blood was so disloyal. Same nigga I struggled with! Same nigga I laid up with in the fucking shelter. Nigga had nothing but larceny in his heart. But why? What the hell I do to dude to cause him to hate so tough? I guess the saying is true. If a nigga ain't number one, he'll always want to be. I just expected such bitchness from Reek.

My head hit the headrest and I tossed the papers on the floor. I turned my head a little, eying the exit to the police station. I was waiting on my lil' mama to walk out. I heard what happened and I knew she was fucking losing it. I needed to get her the fuck away from all of this. I'm chartering us a jet to get the hell out of Michigan. We need some time off. I didn't want to admit it, but I've done exactly what I didn't want to do. Tainted her. She was pure as fuck before she fell for a nigga. Now it's my duty to restore her. I can't have her out here with a cold heart like me. The first kill is always the hardest, but soon after, the shit is like taking a walk through the park. I couldn't let her get to that point in life.

The exit doors opened and what I saw made a nigga's blood boil. Her parents were walking with her, shouting and throwing their arms in the air. Storm walked with them with her head down, arms wrapped around herself. She didn't have on a coat or anything. Couldn't they see she was distraught? Why not be fucking supportive and console her? Can't they understand that's what she needs right now? I let out a deep sigh and snatched my seatbelt off.

I grabbed her bomber jacket from the backseat, and hopped out the whip. As soon as Carlyle saw me approaching with the mug on my face, he jogged over to me with his hands up. He wanted me to stay in the car. Fuck I look like?

"Mr. Williams, it is against my ad—

"Fuck out of here, Carlyle," I said as I pushed past him.

Mack went ballistic. On some real shit, I'm bout ready to end this niggas life. What the fuck is he here for anyway? Shorty ain't fucking with him anymore. Storm looked up at me with sad, tired eyes. Whatever her parents were bitching about didn't matter. In that moment, all I saw was her. All I gave a fuck about was the pretty lil' mama I stared at who looked to have the weight of the world on her shoulders.

I opened my arms as I approached her. Mack grabbed her arm and Storm jerked away. In that moment, I snapped and did the unthinkable. I went for the gun on my waist but Carlyle stopped me before I could pull it out. I didn't give a fuck about being in front of a police station. Didn't give a fuck about the cameras out there. Didn't even give a fuck about the three police officers not too far away. I didn't like the nigga putting his hands on her.

I shot him a cold look and said, "Don't touch her, my mans. Keep yo fucking hands to yourself."

Storm's mom yelled, "Excuse me—

"No disrespect, ma'am. My problem ain't even with you. It's with this fuck nigga," I said as I pointed my finger in Mack's face.

I pulled Storm into me and she buried her face in my chest as I wrapped the jacket around her. I looked down at her and told her she was good. I told her not to worry about shit else. Her body relaxed and we turned and walked away. Ignored the fact that Mack was standing there giving me the coldest death stare

I've ever received. The nigga hated me and the only one to blame was himself.

*

"Where you wanna go brown skin," I asked Storm as I lathered her bath sponge with showergel and ran it over her shoulders.

She shrugged. Storm hadn't said much. We got to the crib about twenty minutes ago. Our first stop was to Receiving Hospital to get her hand stitched up. As soon as we stepped foot in the house, I ran her some bath water.

"Storm," I called out to her after noticing her eyes wandering off.

"Huh," she said, looking back at me.

I dropped the sponge in the water and said, "You gon' be alright lil' mama?"

She pulled her knees up to her chest and nodded, "Just a lot to swallow right now. Too much."

I nodded, "I get it—

"Don't you want to know what I found out?"

I frowned, "What you mean?"

She leaned her head back and stared at the ceiling, "I found out a lot."

TALE 3   MISS CANDICE

I scratched my head, "Nah lil' mama we ain't gotta talk about that shit right now. I'm trying to get you the fuck up out of Michigan for a few days."

She looked at me and said, "Tank. That was Dawson. He sent him to the house."

I gritted my teeth and said, "Storm... baby... we ain't gotta—

"Joslyn was calling you earlier to tell you everything. If I would—

"Stop talking about the shit, Storm! I don't want that shit on yo mind right now. What I want is for you to enjoy your bath and tell a nigga where you wanna vacay to."

She flinched, "I just thought you—

I grabbed her. Pulled her to her feet and held her. Didn't give a fuck about her wet body soaking my tee up. I just wanted her to stop. I needed lil' mama to stop thinking about what happened. It was like the shit consumed her. She knew I didn't want to talk about it but she kept at it. A nigga felt bad for yelling though.

"I'm sorry, Vice. I know she was your friend. But I had to—

"Shhh, just stop shorty, damn!"

I couldn't give a fuck less about her murking Joslyn. I was just happy shit wasn't the other way around. Had that been the case, a nigga would've lost his mind on some one hundred shit. I needed Storm out here. Although we met less than a year ago, I couldn't imagine life without her. How the fuck was I living before her?

"Fiji," said Storm.

I looked down at her, "Fiji what?"

"That's where I want to go."

"Aight, bet. Fiji it is."

She gave me a half smile and I told her I'd be back. I had to get shit together for our trip. I left the bathroom and sat in the living room, on the chaise. I pulled my phone from my jeans, and noticed the many missed calls and texts. What stood out to me was the fact that my auntie, Dawson's mom, hit me up five times. I shook my head and called Reek back.

He answered on the first ring, "Found him."

"That was fast," I said as I held the phone to my ear with my shoulder.

"It was easy."

I started to break a blunt down, "Any names?"

"Fuck no."

"Witnesses?"

"Squeaky clean, bro."

"Aight, brodie," I told him as I licked the blunt paper.

"Bet," said Reek before we end the call.

So much was said without actually being said. Dawson's body was found and there were no suspects.

I sat the phone on the couch and rolled my blunt up. A nigga had to fire up! Like I said before, I couldn't give a fuck less about murking Dawson off. What bothered me was speaking to my auntie about the shit. Dawson was her prized possession. And all Auntie was about to do is blame me for his death. She constantly told me that if Dawson died behind this drug shit, it was on me. Hell yeah it was on me. I took the niggas life; fuck nigga should've thought twice about crossing me. Cuz knew off top about the animal shit I be on when it comes to mothafuckas betraying me. I guess the nigga felt ballzy enough to go against the grain anyway. Look at em now though.

I lit my blunt and took a long pull from it. Fiji. Fuck yeah. Me and my lil mama deserved some time away. Shit had been far too hectic. I needed Storm to be around something other than this mess. Brown skin was changing right before my eyes. I didn't need that. I wanted her pure, and innocent like she was the first moment I laid eyes on her. Shorty wasn't about this gangsta shit period! Now all fucking with a nigga did was taint her.

"What we about to eat? I'm starving," said Storm plopping down on my lap. She snuggled closer to me and wrapped her arms around my neck.

I took a pull from the blunt said, "I see you're feeling better, brown skin."

She looked up at me and smiled, "Being with you has that effect on me, the bath helped too." She looked at the fiery red tip on my blunt and asked, "Can I hit it?"

"For what? You don't blaze up brown skin," I leaned over and put the blunt in an ashtray. Then I rubbed my hands down my face, "Hell naw you can't. Don't ever ask me that shit again."

"Damn, meanie," she said as she playfully nudged me in the chest with her elbow. "Anyway, are we eating or what?"

I'm happy the shock of killing Joslyn is obviously subsiding but she bugging. I can't believe lil mama had the audacity to ask me to hit the blunt. I was still tripping off of that shit. She was doing too fucking much. I was rubbing off on her and I hated the shit, to be honest. I was doing exactly what I didn't want to do – changing her and not in a way I wanted to.

"You be chiefing with Jai?"

Storm frowned and said, "Calm down, Vice. No, I don't. I was just asking because the shit smelled good. Relax."

I nodded and said, "We can order some shit real quick. I'm getting ready to charter the jet. We dipping before the sun rise."

She sat up and finger combed her hair, "Alright, that's cool. I need to call my folks before we leave." She rolled her eyes, "They really tripping."

"What you expect brown skin, baby? Just don't let the shit stress you out. I already stopped Jai from calling, I don't want to do the same thing to yo people's."

"Why did you do that?," she asked with an attitude.

I picked the blunt back up and hit it, "Because she was calling to be nosey. I'm not tryna have you constantly reliving that shit. Fuck you mean? You experienced some traumatic shit, lil mama. I want you to push that shit in the back of your mind, aight?"

She nodded and grabbed my phone off the table, "Pizza?"

"Pizza sounds good, lil mama."

I was in a shitty mood, I can admit that. More so because of the fact that she went through what she went through because of me. I was trying like a mothafucka to keep her away from it all but I've done the exact opposite. What bothered me was that none of it seemed to bother her. She was willing to keep fucking with a nigga despite it all. Shorty's been jumped, disowned by her peoples, kidnapped, and almost killed, all in such a short period of time. She's still here though.

She could've walked away a long time ago. Who the fuck am I? We've been kicking it for under a year – lil mama don't owe me shit. But look at her. Sitting on my lap, ordering a fucking pizza with a smile on her face. She's oblivious to the fact that shit ain't ending with Dawson. What if they next nigga who decides to hate me is worse? It'd fuck me up if anything else happened to her. I hated that she was allowing the love she has for me to cloud her better judgement.

Storm hung up and said, "45 minute wait," she shook her head and jumped off of my lap, "I can't wait that long. Did you go grocery shopping?" she sucked her teeth and waved me off, "I know you didn't. Hopefully there's—

I stood up and pulled her into my chest, "Do you really peep what you're getting yourself into, Storm?"

"What are you talking about, crazy?"

"I'm serious. Think for a second, brown skin. Push that love shit in the back of your mind and think. You really wanna—

"Stop! I know what it is, and every risk associated with loving you. I just don't give a fuck, aight?"

I looked down at her, "You—

"Stop Vice, okay? I know what I'm doing. There's nothing you can do to push me away. You're stuck with me despite your fear of something happening to me again. I know what you're trying to do."

I let her go and she walked into the kitchen. I sat back on the couch, pulling from my blunt. She's right. I was trying to push her away. I wanted her to tell me she couldn't handle it. On the low, I wanted what happened to her earlier to cause her so much stress she wouldn't have a choice but to leave me. I love lil' mama on some serious shit. But I can't be worried about her wellbeing 24/7, 365!

I watched her maneuver around the kitchen like life was grand. Like she didn't just stab a bitch up over a dozen times. She told me she felt better because she was with me. Thing is though, being with me was bad for her. She needed to be as far as possible away from me.

"Pack your luggage," I told her after joining her in the kitchen.

She jumped on top of the counter and opened her arms for me, "Come here, baby."

I smiled, and stood in between her legs, "Yo, what the fuck are you eating?"

She giggled and said, "This is all we have here."

"Mayonnaise and pickles though, Storm?"

She shrugged, "The struggle is real."

TALE 3   MISS CANDICE

As I stared into her brown eyes, guilt washed over me. It ate me up inside, but I wasn't boarding that jet with her. As much as I needed her to level me out, I knew I was no good for her. And I gave a fuck about her more than myself. If I kept her around, knowing the risk, that'd be selfish of me.

*

After we ate, she fell asleep. I was in my office, sitting at my desk, tapping the ink pen against my chin. I had to figure out a way to get her on that jet without me. I was about to be on some fuck shit, but it's what's best. She needs time to think. All being in my presence will do is have her thinking being with me is what's best for her.

Since we've been kicking it, I've stressed to her how I didn't want her involved in this life. But it seemed like the more I tried to keep her away from it, the more she wanted it. Granted, there was nothing she could do about Joslyn jumping her, nor being kidnapped but she was too fucking accepting of it all.

I sat up and wrote a simple note: *Think Storm. That's what I want you to do. Don't let the love you have for a nigga cloud your better judgement. Is this really what you want? You really wanna fuck with a nigga, knowing anytime that some shit like what happened today can pop off again? Love yourself enough to make the right decision– Vice.*

I put it in an envelope and sat it on the desk. Afterward, I chartered a private jet. Dude told me he'd be at the landing spot within an hour. I stood up, stretched, grabbed the note off the desk and joined Storm in the bedroom.

She was sleeping so peaceful. Beautiful as fuck. Never in my life had I laid eyes on someone more beautiful. Lil' mama had me so in my feelings that I even considered saying fuck what I planned to do. I wanted to hop on the jet, and vacay with her. But I couldn't. That would be some selfish shit. Right now, it wasn't about me. It was about her. It'd always be about her. For as long as I live, I will love and think of her. Just from a distance.

I lied next to her, and pulled her closer. She made a few noises before burying her head in my chest. I bit my bottom lip, because a nigga was low key hurt as fuck.

I kissed her on the cheek, "Wake up, beautiful. It's time to go."

She stirred in her sleep and lied on her back. I leaned over her, eying her full breasts, wanting to take one in my mouth. But I knew there wasn't enough time for that freak shit. Still though, a nigga was seriously going to miss the wet, tightness of her pussy. I wanted to hit it at least one more time.

"Storm?"

"Hm?"

I kissed the top of her breast, "We gotta go, lil mama."

She opened her eyes and looked at me. Our eye contact was intense.

"I love you, Vice. More than you'll ever know."

I frowned out of surprise, "Where that come from?"

She smiled and pointed to her chest, "My heart."

I almost got caught up in that love shit, and then remembered – I was cutting her off. I cleared my throat and told her I loved her too, before getting out of the bed. Hell yeah I loved her. So fucking much that doing this shit was eating at me. I didn't want to live in this cold ass world without her. I needed her. She was my escape from the fucked up reality I lived in. But she had to do better. Fuck it, I was willing to let another nigga luck up. That thought alone filled me with rage and I bit down on my lips.

I looked over my shoulder at her and said, "Get up, we gotta go."

4

STORM

Is this the mothafucking thanks I get? I held him down! I'm the reason he's not rotting in jail right mothafucking now! But did he seem to give a damn? No! He walked away from me. Walked away from the love he so called had for me. Vice expected me to just get on the jet without him. He really expected me to go to Fiji with a smile on my face like he didn't just break my heart into pieces. That's not what happened. I stood there, outside of the jet, hugging myself to keep warm as tears poured down my face. He didn't seem to care about that neither. Why was he doing this to me?

Vice don't know how to love anybody, bitch, don't let that game fool you. Joslyn's irritating ass voice echoed through my mind and I thought, maybe she was right. I never second guessed the love Vice had for me until now. He was hell bent on making me his woman. He promised not to hurt me. But now, he was doing just that.

"Take care of yourself li—

I yelled, "Don't tell me to take care of myself like you give a fuck, Vice! Why are you doing this to me!?"

He stood there, hands stuffed in the pocket of his Polo coat emotionless. Vice was unmoved by my tears which bothered the fuck out of me.

"I'm not doing anything to you, Storm. You're doing this to yourself. If you just hop on the j—

I jumped in his face and grabbed his hand. I placed it on my chest and said, "You feel that shit!?

He backed away, trying to pull his hand away but I firmly held onto it, "Come on, brown skin."

I yelled, "Do you feel the way my heart is racing, Vice? Do you?" He nodded and I continued, "You...you told me I couldn't cut you off remember? Now I'm telling you the same thing! We were made for one another! You're the...the balance a young woman like me needs."

Vice bit down on his bottom lip and I allowed him to pull his hand away. I thought things were going my way. But when he walked away, my stomach dropped simultaneously to me dropping to my knees. He was breaking up with me. Why? This is too much. Too much. I can't take any more pain. Haven't I suffered enough today?

TALE 3   MISS CANDICE

"Vice," I screamed at the top of my lungs as tears and snot fell down my face.

He looked over his shoulder and said, "Your Uber is on its way since you don't want to utilize the jet I got yo—

I threw my Louis Vuitton suitcase at him, "Fuck you Vice! Fuck you! I hate you!"

He stopped in his tracks and stared at me. He looked down at the opened designer luggage and back up at me. Vice started to walk my way but stopped. He sighed and ran his hands down his face.

"Get up, Storm."

I didn't. I sat there on my knees feeling as though I was paralyzed. I couldn't move. The world around me was spinning and I felt sick. I threw up all over the ground, and myself. I was so happy an hour ago. I successfully pushed the thought of killing Joslyn in the back of my mind and decided to just live. After constantly telling myself I did what was necessary, I was okay. I sat in that tub, smiling. The overflowing of love Vice constantly showed me filled me with joy. I was happy. Happy despite the fact that I had gone through more drama because of him. I didn't care. I just wanted to be with him.

I wiped my mouth with the back of my hand as I continued to sit there sobbing uncontrollably. I've never been hurt like this. My ex hurt me but this...this was destroying me. I was embarrassing myself. I knew I looked a complete mess but I didn't care. I no longer had control of myself.

I looked up at Vice who was approaching me and asked, "Why?"

He looked down at me, with sad hazel brown eyes. He didn't want this to be over just as much as I didn't. So why was he hurting me like this? He kneeled down in front of me and wiped my face with his Burberry shirt.

"Stop, brown skin. This shit is eating a nigga up."

He grabbed the back of my head and pulled me into his chest. Vice didn't give a damn about the throw up he was stepping in, that was fucking up his designer shoes. He didn't care about ruining the expensive shirt he wore. He was so selfless when it came to me. So, why was he breaking my heart?

"Why are you doing this to me," I asked as I pulled away.

TALE 3   MISS CANDICE

He grabbed me again, holding me so tight I was having a hard time breathing.

"I don't want to lose you behind this shit, baby. I can't. I won't," he said in my ear.

"You won't, Vice. I promise I'll be ca—

He let me go and said, "This is me being careful. I shouldn't have even fucked with you in the first place. You making this shit hard. But listen... it's happening regardless."

I was tired. Sick and tired so I stopped crying. I pulled myself off the ground and nodded at him, "What am I supposed to do, Vice?"

He stood up, and adjusted his stained jeans before saying, "Forget about me."

Tears were begging to be released from my tear ducts. I held them back until the stinging was unbearable. I silently cried, as I watched him walk away. I looked over my shoulder at the pilot watching and frowned. I was so embarrassed. Especially when the Uber driver pulled up as I was picking up the things that fell out of the luggage from the ground. I bent down and picked up a folded piece of paper.

I unfolded it and read his chicken scratch, while tears fell onto the paper. I didn't give a fuck about what he was saying. How he breaking up with me because he's afraid something will happen? What kind of sense does that make? I could get in this Uber and the driver could crash, killing me. Hell, I could be killed while checking my mail. Death is inevitable. Why not live a little?

"You okay, ma'am," asked the Uber driver after lowering his window.

I looked ahead, watching Vice watching me. The tints on the Challenger were dark but I knew he was watching. He always watched me.

I turned towards the driver and said, "Yeah, give me a second."

He shifted the car in park and said, "Let me help you with your things."

I rolled the carry-on to the Uber, and then tossed the Vuitton duffle bag over my shoulder. I told the driver I'd be right back, and then treaded towards Vice's car. I had a few things to get off of my chest.

When I made it to him, I stood outside of his door. He rolled his window down but didn't even look at me.

"You can't save me from death, Vice. Stop being stupid."

"You want something, baby girl?"

His dismissive tone hurt me. Heated my chest up. I pulled my lips in my mouth and nodded, "You're trying to push me—

"Fuck you want, Storm? Shit! You got the man waiting—

I drew back and said, "No, fuck you Vice! You taking this shit too far! Talking to me like you've lost yo damn mind! You're battling with sh—

"You don't know what a nigga's battling with," said Vice finally turning my way. "Watch out."

"I love you, Vice."

He rolled his window up, and pulled off.

The more I told myself he was only treating me this way because he was afraid of losing me behind the drug game, the more it hurt. I understood where he was coming from but he didn't have to be so rude. I kept my eyes on his car until he was no longer in sight.

With my shoulders slumped over, I walked to the Uber. He met me half way and pat me on the back, "You sure you're okay?"

I nodded and wiped a lone tear from my face, "I'm cool. I just want to go home."

"Let's roll," he said as he opened the door for me.

*

Thirty minutes later, I was home with my face in the toilet bowl throwing my soul up. I've never thrown up so viciously. This break up just happened and it was taking a toll on me. That there showed me just how much he meant to me.

I sat on the bathroom floor, with my arm draped over the toilet. I was bugging. But like I said, I didn't have any control over myself. Right now, love was consuming me. I loved Vice so much that I got lost in him. The type of lost that's just like being found. I found myself in him. I thought this would last forever. Why is it that I have to suffer? Why won't he just leave the game? Aren't I more important?

The ringing of my phone startled me. It was him. I jumped up so fast, I bumped my head on the corner of the sink.

"Fuck," I yelled as I grabbed my forehead. I felt the knot beginning to swell already.

I ran to the living room, where I dropped everything as soon as I hit the door. I fumbled through my Chanel bag until I found it. He hung up before I could answer. I sat on the carpeted floor and called him back as I wiped throw up from my mind with my freehand.

"Hey you just c—

"You home?"

"Ye—

"Alright. I was just checking up on you," he said, cutting me off again.

"Listen, we need to talk."

Silence.

"Hello?"   ˙

Nothing.

I looked at the phone and he had already hung up. I threw my phone across the room and regretted it as soon as it hit the wall and broke into pieces. Is this life? This can't be life. I was being dealt a shitty hand.

5

REEK

"You gone be straight up here by yourself," I asked as I threw my Al Wissam leather on.

She pulled the thick bed comforter over her shoulders, "Yes, I'll be fine. Thanks for sticking around for as long as you did."

I nodded with a smile and told her, "It's cool, sweetie. I enjoyed kicking it with you."

Laila smiled and sat up. She grabbed an ink pen and note pad from the nightstand beside her and scribbled on it. When she handed it to me, my eyes grew big as saucers. I handed it back to her.

"Bro will fuck around and choke me out," I said with a laugh as I waited on her to take the number from my hands.

She didn't know how crazy her fucking brother was. Nigga would probably skin me alive if he even suspected me fucking with his sister. On the other hand though, maybe not. All of this shit was sudden. But still, Laila is off limits. I have too much respect and love for Vice to smash his sis. Since, that's exactly what the fuck I'd end up doing.

She's too fucking bad. As I looked at her, looking back at me my dick grew with excitement. My eyes roamed her body. Laila was lying on her side, hips and ass poking out. Round titties pressing tightly against the thin fabric of her white tank. Man, I'd disrespect the fuck out of that pussy.

"I'm a grown woman, Tyreek, I can talk to whomever I please," said Laila as removed her legs from up under the cover, and sat on side of the bed.

I looked down the thickness of her thighs and wanted to part those juicy mothafuckas with my tongue. I took a step back and adjusted my designer jeans. Baby girl had my dick on stiff and I didn't want her to peep the affect she had on me.

She took the paper from me and stood up. Laila was about 5'5 – the same height as me. She smiled and pulled her lips into her mouth as she slowly approached me. I stuffed my hands in my pocket and asked what the fuck she was doing. Laila stood in front of me and put her hand in my pocket and then quickly removed it.

"Giving you my number. If you don't call me, I'll very upset," she turned around and walked off. My eyes stayed on her round, plump ass until she sat on the bed.

I went in my pocket and sat the number on the nightstand, "I guess I'll just have to live with that then, sweetie." I nodded and turned her goodnight before walking out of the room.

Two hours later, I was at the crib, sitting on side of the bed, slumped over, pulling from a blunt full of Kush. My mind was crowded – felt like I had the weight of the world on my damn shoulders. I took a long drag, inhaling and then exhaling the smoke. A nigga is dumb stressed. Fucking off in this street life will do that to you.

"Baby, you sure you don't want me to stay," said Keesh standing in front of me, running her fingers through my dreads.

I didn't even bother lifting my head. My eyes stayed on the carpeted floor. Hell yeah I wanted her thot ass to go. I only called her over here to drain my balls dry because Laila had done a fucking number on me. That's all Keesh is good for. Vice could joke around about me cuffing this bitch all he wanted to, but that was furthest from the truth. The ho had some good ass pussy and her head game was fire. That's the only reason I kept her around.

"Yeah, I'm sure. Hit that bottom lock," I told her as I grabbed the glass ashtray from my nightstand and put the blunt out.

"Well, call me if you need to talk okay?"

I nodded and she walked out of the room. The only time I called her was when I needed to bust one. This will most likely be our last night together. I had my eyes on someone else.

Earlier, after everything popped off, Vice sent me to his room to check on his sister. His sister? A nigga was dumb bugging off of that. I didn't even know the nigga had any family other than Dawson and his other cousins he was posted in the shelter with. So when he mentioned his sister, I sat there in shock trying to understand what the fuck he was saying. He told me he would explain it all to me later.

As soon as I walked in the room and laid eyes on her, I wanted her to be mine. Laila was dressed in a tan sweater dress, and UGG boots sitting on the couch biting her nails. Although Vice told her I was coming to check on her, she still flinched when I walked in. The bruises and busted lip told me why. Some pussy nigga had laid hands on her. Who would be stupid enough to beat on a bitch as pretty as Laila? Off bat, by looking at her, I knew she had to have some bomb ass pussy.

She nervously smiled at me and introduced herself as Laila. I approached her like a gentleman. I left all that gangsta hood shit at the door. I had to gain her trust. If I came at her on some old gangsta, hood nigga shit she would've been uncomfortable. I didn't know how long I was going to be sitting there with her, so I didn't want things to be awkward.

We kicked it for a few hours before Vice called me off of her. I knew she would try to slip me her number. We were having too much fun for her not to catch feelings. I made her smile and laugh. I obviously made her forget about the bullshit she went through the other night. But as bad as I wanted to take that number, I couldn't. Not until I holla at Vice about it.

*

The next morning I woke up to my phone buzzing. Off rip, I knew it was my OG. I wiped crust from my eyes and grabbed my hitter off the nightstand. Before I answered it, I took notice of the time. *8:42AM.* What could she possibly want so early? A nigga just laid down not too long ago.

"Good morning moms," I answered.

"Good morning, Tyreek. Get on up, and come over."

I shook my head, "For what? It's eight in the morning."

"Your cousin just came to town and the family is getting together. Now, get yo narrow ass on over here."

"Ma...I just—

"I don't give a damn, Tyreek Davis. Now, we haven't seen Luke in years. Y'all use to be best cousins. I bet if I was Vice yo ass—

"Alright, alright. I'll be through there in a minute."

"Okay, Reek baby. I love you. Brang me a pack of Newport's too."

I told her I loved her too and hung up.

I couldn't give a fuck less about Luke being in town. Me and the nigga fell out years ago. Little did the fam know, he left town because of me. I sent his crazy ass packing. There was no way in hell I was about to allow what happened to Vice happen to me. I noticed the larceny in Luke's heart before this here business was as profitable as it is now.

Damn near my whole family stayed in that shelter me and Vice met at. Times were hard as hell back then. In addition to my sister and me, moms had my three cousins staying with us too. I remember the day like it was yesterday.

We were all sitting in the living room, joking around, watching BET when the bailiff came through with the eviction notice and two other niggas in tow. I was seventeen and wasn't having that shit. I didn't know what was going on. Mom's was crying trying to block their paths. Off rip, when the tears fell from her eyes, I snapped. I pushed her aside and told them to get out. But when the bailiff shoved the eviction notice in my face, I fell back. I didn't have a fucking choice. We were being evicted and if I did anything else, I could've been thrown in jail.

So my cousins and I took our asses on the front porch, waiting. We stood there with our heads down, embarrassed as everyone in the hood watched what was happening.

By the time they were finished, all of our shit was sitting on the front lawn. I had to stop a few crackhead mothafuckas from taking shit. For the first night, we all slept on the front porch. Thank God it was spring time. Mom's was too proud to go to the shelter. After that first night, we didn't have a choice though. The cops came and told us we had to vacate the premises.

Mom's called gramps and he paid to have our shit put in storage. Nigga didn't even offer to let us stay there. At that moment, I realized why moms didn't want to ask for help. Gramps and them were funny acting as hell. That same night, we went to the shelter. OG promised we'd only be there for a week. A week turned into two months. We didn't get the fuck up out of there until Vice put me on. The first rack I made went to copping us a crib.

Once Luke noticed how tight me and Vice were, the nigga started to subliminally hate. Even after I put him on, I was throwing him major bread to get his gear up. But that didn't seem to be enough. A year passed and he was still on the same fuck shit. I came across an out of town plug, and out him on it. I presented Luke with a sweet ass deal, and just like a sucker, he took it. He didn't give a fuck about leaving his little sisters behind. All he cared about was making money. His main focus was making more bread than Vice and I. If I would've kept the nigga around something was bound to happen. So I nipped that shit in the bud before he could even think of a perfect scheme to fuck us over.

The nigga is only back to floss. But what he don't know is, since he left I got my cake up. Majorly. I don't floss like most niggas. Didn't even cop a crib out the hood. But that doesn't mean there's a paper shortage. Hell naw it's not. I'm just more comfortable out here. I can't stand being around white people. The shit makes me antsy as hell. I planned on stunting just for the goofy nigga. Right now though, I need to get a lil more sleep.

I turned my ringer off, and set my alarm for noon.

*

Hours later I was up and speeding down i-94 in my cherry red Camaro. The heat was on blast, and the stereo was too. I was in a hood nigga mood so I had Jeezy, Thug Motivation, banging. I didn't want to see the weak ass nigga but mom's was on some other shit so I had to roll through. She hit me up about five times. I didn't even bother returning the call. All she was going to do is yell. She'll be straight when I put this box of Newport's in her hands.

I didn't leave the hood, but I made sure moms did. She was sitting comfortably in a four bedroom house out in Sterling Heights, MI. My twin sister Tyreeka stayed there too, with her twin boys. I didn't visit as much as I liked too and that was because I'm a busy nigga. Ain't shit easy or sweet about the drug life. Hell, a nigga was lucky as fuck to get some sleep in last night.

Fifteen minutes after hopping off the freeway, I was parking in the circular driveway in front of mom's crib, behind an ugly ass Hummer. The driveway was to capacity so I knew my fam was on the inside. The Hummer though? Shit had Luke written all over it.

I grabbed the box of 'Port's off the passenger seat and hopped out after unplugging my phone from the AUX. Before I got to the door, I heard the music and loud laughter. These mothafuckas were really celebrating this dude's arrival like he deserved the shit.

I twisted the doorknob, and as expected, it was unlocked. They didn't even hear me come in. As I walked down the hallway, towards the laughter, I shook my head. Mom's even cooked for this weak ass nigga. Finally, I made it to the family room where everyone were crowded around who I'm assuming was Luke.

"I'm so happy to have you here, sweetie," said my mom's.

I walked over to the crowd and all eyes fell on me. I didn't even bother saying wassup to Luke who had a bad ass yellow bone sitting on his lap. I handed my momma the box of cigarettes, kissed her on the cheek, and walked away. I joined Tyreeka who was sitting on the other side of the room, with one of my nephews in her lap.

"Reek! I know you ain't walking in my house being a rude ass," yelled my moms as I walked off.

I looked over my shoulder and spoke to my aunts and uncles. Never even acknowledging Luke.

"You don't see your cou—

"Yeah I see the nigga. Wassup Luke?"

Luke chuckled and said, "Tech. Why you gotta disrespect me, Reek?"

"What the hell I look like calling you Tech like you some gangsta? Nigga please!"

I'm usually a laid back, mellow nigga but Luke put me in a fucked up headspace. I swear, the nigga is a straight up hater. The family is just blinded by the fake ass façade he puts on for them. I'm the only person in this room, besides him, that knows the real deal. Tech, as he likes to call himself, ain't a fucking gangsta. He's only getting money because I put him on that out of town connect. Otherwise, he'd be a bum ass nigga out here or dead. The boy had some serious animosity in his heart for Vice and I.

"What is wrong with you boys? Y'all were so close," yelled my momma with wrinkled eyebrows.

"Were so close, ma," I said as I grabbed Javion from Tyreeka's lap. "Past tense. I don't fuc—

"Watch yo damn mouth, Tyreek Davis!"

"Don't worry about it, auntie. Cuz just feeling some type of way," said Luke as he grabbed onto the thick bitch on his lap, "We just got some rapping to do. Ain't that right, Ty?"

I waved him off and turned my back on them. I sat beside my sister and asked her how she been. Me and Ty use to be tight as hell. We're still close. I just don't come around like I use to. Drama was at an all-time high for Vice and I. Now, it seems like we've tied up all loose ends and can finally relax a little.

"What happened between y'all," whispered Tyreeka.

"Nigga's a bitch, sis," I said as my nephew bounced on my lap, "My bad neph."

She lightly punched me in the arm, "Now if he start cursing I'm beating you." Ty laughed, "But forreal bro, what happened?"

"I'll hit your line letter, sis."

We sat there talking for about twenty minutes. Ty filled me in on what was going on in her life. I applaud the fuck out of my sister. She's a single parent of twins, doing better than most. She holds down a full time job, and goes to school for Physical Therapy. My mom helps out with babysitting but that's all. I throw sis bread every now and then. Also, I pay her utility bills monthly. She refuses the help but I help anyway. I witnessed first-hand how difficult being a single parent is. I don't want her thinking she don't have help. We didn't have that when we were growing up.

The entire time, Luke kept staring at me. Swear if this nigga becomes a problem I won't hesitate taking him out. Fuck him. I couldn't understand why we were celebrating the weak ass nigga.

My phone rung, *Bro.*

I sat Javion on Ty's lap and slid the green phone over and said, "Wassup bro?"

"Where you at, brodie?"

"Mom's crib. What it is?"

TALE 3   MISS CANDICE

"I'm about to swing through. What's popping over there?"

"Luke touched down yesterday."

"Aight, bet. I'm on my way."

We hung up and I shook my head. I never told Vice about the feelings I had about Luke. I didn't tell bro that I thought he was flakey on some disloyal shit. Simply because I know Vice and bro would've took him out no questions asked. He wouldn't have given a fuck about Luke being my blood. Shit, look at what he did to his own flesh and blood. So I did the only rational thing. I sent Luke away. Vice thought cuz found his own out-of-state connect. Furthest thing from the truth.

As I sat there rubbing on my beard, I figured it was time to put that bug in his ear. With the way Luke was mugging it felt like something was about to pop off. I don't even consider the pussy nigga family anymore. Weak ass nigga over there smiling, staring at me like I'm supposed to be intimidated. When he left I was young. Now I'm a grown ass nigga with a few bodies in the closet. I won't hesitate to split his fucking melon.

I stood up and walked over to the food table. My stomach was growling, and as much as I wanted to be on some antisocial shit I couldn't ignore the rumbling.

As I stood there putting Mac-n-cheese on my plate, I felt a hand on my shoulder. I looked to my left and gritted my teeth before roughly smacking his hand off of me.

"What's wrong, blood," asked Luke, piling wingdings on his plate.

I moved along to the baked beans and said, "You nigga. Fuck you around here for? I thought I told you not to show yo face in the D anymore."

He chuckled and slammed a glob of black eyed peas on my plate knowing I hated them shits, "I'm not that same nigga." He picked a wing ding up from his plate and bit it, "I heard y'all making major moves out here. I need a piece of the pie."

I picked my plate up and slammed it on top of his before turning his way, "You betta get the fuck from round here on that fuck shit nigga!"

I was hot. Heated. Who the fuck this nigga think he is? Come through trying to be on some animal shit like I wasn't raised in the fucking jungle. The music was blasting so no one knew what was transpiring. Tyreeka was watching though. She held both of nephews on her hips, watching with concern. I nodded to her and she sat down. I didn't want her worrying when I'm clearly unfazed.

Luke wiped his mouth with a napkin and faced me with a smile, "You aight, *blood*? You seem a little shook."

My nose flared with anger, "Never shook my nigga!" I smiled, "I'm cooler than the other side of the pillow. You don't want to take it there, my nigga. But, if you do I won't mind taking it there for real." I smirked and exposed the burner on my waist, "Feel me?"

Luke looked down at it and then back up at me, "Small thing to a giant. You better do yo research *blood*. I'm not that soft nigga you sent away. I got clout fuck boy." He looked past me and said, "Yo boss here." He laughed, "Flunky ass nigga." Luke said before walking away, bumping me in the process.

I grabbed the nigga by the back of his shirt and snatched him back. I didn't realize how much force I used until he went crashing into the food table, knocking everything off. Now that... grabbed everyone's attention. The music stopped and everything. Moms looked at me with so much fire in her eyes that I had to turn away.

"What the hell is going on," she yelled.

"Whoa, what's good brodie?" asked Vice with a mug on his face.

"Sorry auntie, this nigga really in his feelings," said Luke as he stood up knocking collard greens off of his True Religion jeans.

I nodded at Vice and said, "Shit's good bro. We'll rap abo—

"I told you to watch your mouth Tyreek," yelled my momma before turning to Vice, "And good afternoon Vice. Walking in my house without speaking!"

Vice turned to her and gave her a hug, the whole time his eyes were on Luke, "Sorry ma. How you doing today, beautiful?"

My momma smiled and said, "I'm fine, son." She glared at me, "About to beat the hell out of your friend! I know he better pick that damn food up! He better be happy we all ate already!"

I turned around and started to pick food up.

"Wassup, Vice," said Luke.

TALE 3   MISS CANDICE

I looked over my shoulder and he was wearing a grin with his hand extended to Vice.

Vice looked at his hand and then back up at him, "Ay bro, let's chop it up in the whip." Moms shot him a look and he said, "When you finish up in here, of course."

Bro knew something was off. Any other time, he would've slapped hands with Luke. No matter the case, bro had my back just like I had his.

"Fa sho," I replied.

Luke waved Vice off as he walked away, "You niggas really in y'all feelings today." He paused, "Aye, let's roll Chantelle."

The bitch he was with stood up and walked over to his side while seductively eying me before grabbing his hand.

I chuckled and finished cleaning the food up before joining bro outside.

As soon as I hopped in the whip and closed the door, he passed me a blunt.

"Exactly what the fuck a nigga need," I told him as the smoke choked me up a little.

Vice turned the heat up and said, "Fuck wrong with Luke?"

I passed the blunt back to him and said, "Bitch nigga goes by the name of Tech now," I laughed, "Cuzzo think he's a gangsta fa real!"

He hit the blunt and glanced, "Nigga must've hit his head a few times, coming at us sideways. Fuck happened to him? He grew a pair, uh?"

"Apparently bro," I paused, "I need to keep it one hundred with you though. I sent cuz off back then. I put 'em on that Missouri connect because he was on some envious flakey, shit. I had to get him as far as—

"Then you should've sent a bullet between his eyes," said Vice, fumbling with the radio. "And then," he looked at me, "Then we wouldn't be having issues with the fuck boy right?"

I shifted in my seat, "True enough, brodie. But peep, I won't hesitate to burn his ass if n—

"Damn right you won't because if you do," he took a pull from the l, "We both know I won't hesitate to."

I sighed, "Shit, here you go!"

Vice didn't say anything else. Nigga didn't even pass the blunt back to me. He sat back in his seat after adjusting the volume to the radio. The fuck was this nigga on? This nigga was really zoning out to Fab You Make Me Better. I looked at him from the corner of my eye and he was bobbing his head.

You plus me, it equals better math.
Ya boy a good look but, she my better half.
I'm already bossin', already flossin'.
But why I have the cake if it ain't got the sweet frostin'?
Keepin' me on my A game.
Without havin' the same name
They may flame
But shawty, we burn it up.
The sag in my swag, pep in my step.
Daddy do the Gucci, mami in Giuseppes.
Yes it's a G thing, whenever we swing.
I'mma need Coretta Scott, if I'm gonna be King.

First thing's first, I does what I do.
But everything I am, she's my influ.
I'm already boss, I'm already fly.
But if I'm a star, she is the sky
And when I feel like I'm on top

She give me reason to not stop.
And though I'm hot.
Together we burn it up

"Fuck you on, my nigga," I yelled over the loud music.

Vice took a pull from the blunt, glanced at me, and then at the blunt.

He was on some other shit. The niggas so damn unpredictable, I was a bit iffy. Never in my life have I seen the nigga on this tip.

The song ended and he turned the radio back down.

"Brown skin got a nigga vexed out here," said Vice looking out the window.

"What happened?"

"Fucking with me is dangerous. And it's obvious that Luke on some other shit. Nigga wouldn't be a problem if you did what you should've did. But since you didn't I'm glad I ended shit with her. Dawg... I give a fuck about lil' mama way too much to let something else happen to her because of my shit," he took a pull from the blunt, "Fuck no."

I nodded and shifted in my seat, "Chill nigga. If need be, I'll take care of the pussy myself. But, I feel you bro. This is a dirty game, yo." He passed the blunt back to me and I said, "But on the real, bro." I smiled, "You ain't gone be able to leave her lil' ass alone."

Vice never came at me about a female. Storm must be special as fuck to him. Before he met her he was a 'fuck bitches, get money' type of cat. Now he's sitting here in his feelings. Nigga even switched his music up and he's not even an R&B type cat.

.

Usually, I'd be on some joke type shit but I could tell bro was serious as hell about 'brown skin'. Still, I was shocked. Every time we linked up it was always about business. Nigga never opened up to me. Seemed like since Dawson turned out to be a snake, he trusted me a lil' mo. Made a nigga comfortable as hell. Despite the fact that I always seemed laid back about the dumb shit he did, the nigga was intimidating. Simply because he was a ticking time bomb. It felt good to just be on some chill, kicking back shit.

Vice flashed me a mischievous grin, "Real spit. She got me on some other shit huh, nigga?"

I nodded, "Never in my life have I seen you on this tip. To be honest, the shit kinda weird."

He laughed, "Weird for me too bro," he waved me off, "Fuck all of that shit though. A nigga just had a moment. We need to figure out what we gon' do about your cousin." I passed him the blunt and he pulled from it before saying, "Gone fuck around and have to give him the Dawson treatment."

I nodded in agreement. Because despite the blood we shared, I simply didn't give a fuck.

6.

VICE

I needed eyes on Luke, or Tech as he likes to call himself. I'll never call the pussy Tech. That type of name is fit for G's and that ain't even him. Well, it wasn't when he left this bitch. It had been a week since that shit popped off at Reeks OG crib and the nigga was still heavy on my mental. I don't know what type of tip he on these days, which is why I'm tryna put a tail on him. I'll have to pull one of my young niggas from a house to keep an eye on him. Probably one of those hot headed niggas from the six. Give 'em something to do. Make 'em feel more important than they actually are.

I was heading that way right now anyway. Heat and Blade Icewood blasting. A nigga was trying to keep the gangsta alive. The shit that was going on between Storm and I had me on some R&B, in love, in my feelings type shit. I had to shake that with the quickness. I kept telling myself that leaving her was for the best. But I needed her lil' brown sexy ass. I've had to stop myself from texting and calling her on numerous occasions. I ended up having to delete her from my contacts.

I pulled into the parking lot of Chet's liquor store and hopped out. A panhandler was standing outside, so I went in my North Face coat and handed her a knot of money. I know what the struggle feels like so whenever I see someone down and out, I help. I don't even know how much was in the knot, and I really didn't give a fuck. She'll probably shoot it all up and I didn't give a fuck about that neither. If that's the case, I'll get the money right back anyway since it'll be my drugs she cop.

I walked in the store and a group of young niggas at the counter gave me head nods. I nodded back at them and headed to the back of the store to the freezers. A nigga was thirsty as fuck. A cold ass Pepsi would hit the spot.

As I'm standing in the back of the store, I heard someone walk in.

"Get that bum bitch from in front of your store, man," he yelled. "Bitch out there smelling like a whole toilet full of shit."

The young niggas cracked up and I didn't find anything he said funny. Especially since I recognized the nigga's voice as Luke's. He knew the struggle all too well to be making fun of somebody who's in a situation similar to what the fuck he was in.

I walked to the front of the store with a mug on my face, "You speaking like a nigga that's always been getting it."

Luke turned around, leaning up against the counter, "What's up cuz?"

I looked down at his hand and turned my nose up, "Fuck is you doing over in my hood, pussy nigga?"

Luke giggled and looked at the group of young niggas expecting them to giggle with him. Thing is, these niggas were my niggas. They knew me and to know me is to respect me. If I told one of these young cats to put hands on Luke that's exactly what they'd do. They looked at him with a mug sicker than the one I wore on my face.

"Ahhh, I get it," said Luke as he stood up straight, "These yo lil' niggas huh?"

I sat my Pepsi on the counter, "Ay, Franky, let me get a couple swishers," I turned to Luke, "My hood, my niggas. Fuck you thought? Now I asked you, what the fuck you doing over here?"

The young cats that were once leaning on the counter was now standing behind me. Hands on their burners, ready for war. Luke didn't look intimidated though, and that bothered me. The Luke I remembered was a cur. He didn't like confrontation which is why he always sat in houses for me back in the day.

He held his hands up, "A nigga just need a couple blacks. Nothing more, *fam.*"

I smirked and bumped him on my way out of the store, "Aight nigga, if I catch you around here on fuck shit again, acting like you been had money, like you ain't from the bottom...circumstances will be different. *Fam.*"

He stumbled a little and said, "Yeah okay, my nigga."

I looked over my shoulder before walking out of the door. After getting a glimpse of the menacing grin on his face I knew off bat I had to end the nigga pronto. Luke...Tech...whoever the fuck he thought he was is going to be a problem I don't need in my life right now.

*

Hours later, I was stepping out of the shower, drenched and drying off. I had a few runs to make. First stop was to scoop Reek up. We had to sort shit out. The discussion of what we were going to do about Tech was a must. The nigga still walking around breathing didn't sit well with me. All I saw was hate in his eyes when he looked at me. The nigga wanted me dead so it was a must that I caught up with that fuck nigga before he got me.

As I was slipping my Polo boxer briefs on there was a knock on my door. Whoever it was didn't call or shit, so they were overstepping major ass boundaries. I had pistols stashed all around the crib, and grabbed one from underneath the medicine cabinet.

"Yo, who that?" I asked as I approached the front door.

"Me."

I stopped dead in my tracks and mumbled, "Fuck."

Storm was here. She wasn't supposed to be though. I missed the fuck up out of brown skin. I wanted to see her but I knew better. I needed to push her away. As much as I didn't want to hurt her, I didn't have a choice.

"Go home, lil' mama," I told her as I sat in the chair next to the door.

"Open the door, Vice," she yelled as she banged.

"Gone on home, a nigga ain't fucking with you," saying those words to her ate me up. I bit down on my bottom lip out of frustration.

She was silent but I knew she was still standing there. I stood up and leaned my back against the door. I wanted to hold her in my arms. Wanted to bury my face in her neck and inhale. I knew she smelled good. Storm always smelled good. I turned around and looked through the peephole. From what I could tell, she looked good too. Good as fuck. Looked like her hair was just done up, and her makeup was flawless. A nigga's heart went soft and I grabbed the doorknob but stopped myself from twisting it.

"I miss you," she said as her voice cracked.

I shook my head, "For what? I'm not thinking about you shorty. Understand that that shit is over, aight? Fuck out of here!"

I had to be an ass. As much as I didn't want to, I had no choice. I was bad for her. But fuck, lil' mama was good for me. I needed her. She just didn't need me. I watched her as she hugged herself, rubbing her arms to keep warm. She was cold. Of course she was. Storm didn't have on a jacket. She stood on the porch in a short ass sweater dress, and those ugly ass furry boots.

"Where's your coat? You tryna get sick or some shit, brown skin?"

TALE 3　　　　　MISS CANDICE

As soon as the words left my lips I regretted it. She knew I was watching her. She knew I cared. I hated how I couldn't mask the fact that I cared. I gave a fuck for sure.

Storm's eyes shot up to the peephole and she slowly approached the door, "You miss me just as much as I miss you."

I didn't respond. I stood there staring at her through the peephole as my heart pounded against my chest. She had me on some sucker shit. I loved her. I've never yearned for someone so much. I wanted to touch her. Wanted to feel her soft ass body against my rough one. Most of all though, I wanted to smell her. Wanted to kiss her full, soft lips. Shorty had me under a spell. I was addicted to her. A nigga needed rehab like a mothafucka.

I shook my head and opened up.

She lifted her head, and a tear fell from her eye.

Storm's full lips curled up into a smile and she said, "Hi."

I nodded, "Wassup brown skin?"

She opened her arms and I inched in closer to her. As soon as we embraced each other, I buried my face in her neck and inhaled. Deeper than ever. I missed the fuck out of her smell. She draped her arms over my shoulders and rubbed the nape of my neck. Her hands were soft as hell.

We stood there, hugging each other for about ten minutes not giving a fuck about the freezing cold beating against our skin. . A nigga was dead ass standing in the door, in thirty degree weather, in nothing but boxer briefs. On the real, I wasn't even cold. Her body temperature was fire; she ignited my soul. Never in my life, had I spoke like this. When I was around Storm I was a different me. Some would say a better me. I didn't know. However, what I did know is that I didn't like how weak she made me feel.

"Don't do that to me again," said Storm after we finally closed the door and sat on the couch. "I nearly lost my mind."

I didn't respond. Mainly because I didn't know what I was doing, or what was to become of us. I couldn't fuck with her. That was for sure, but I had to fuck with her. I couldn't help but fuck with her. I didn't need to. I needed her to stay away from me. Especially since Luke on some ho shit.

"Are you okay?," Storm asked as she straddled me with my face in her hands.

My eyes landed on the deep split in her dress. Her titties looked better than ever. I ran my finger over the ampleness of her breast and she closed her eyes. I looked up at her and mumbled 'damn'. Lil' mama too fucking cold. She was wearing too much makeup but still, she was beautiful. Shorty was on her extra shit. She came over here with intentions of fucking with my mental. She wanted me under her spell. Thing is, I was already under it and dressing provocatively wearing hella makeup didn't cause that.

I ran my large hands over her hips, and hiked her dress up over her waist. She happily obliged. Brown skin wanted this shit just as much as I did. If the intensity behind her eye contact as she pulled my dick from my boxers, wasn't enough confirmation, then the dampness of her lace panties was.

As I lightly ran my fingers over her clitoris through the thin fabric of her lace thongs, she moaned for me to wait and I covered her mouth with mines. The last thing I wanted to do was talk. I was afraid that if I did, I'd fuck this up with some rude shit. I didn't want her in my life but I needed her. I couldn't live without her. Getting her out of my mind was proving to be harder than I expected.

Storm wrapped her arms around my neck and matched my intensity. Her mouth was so sweet, and wet. At an instant, I wanted her pussy on my tongue. Her mouth might've been sweet and wet, but best believe the pussy was sweeter...wetter.

I pulled away from the kiss, and snatched her thongs clean off. My roughness caused her to gasp in surprise. Before she could react to the slight pain ripping her thongs off, I had her on my shoulders. Shaved pussy in my face. Her thighs were drenched in her juices, wetting up the sides of my face. Before dipping my tongue in, I inhaled. *Got damn.* Most intoxicating scent I've even inhaled in my life.

I opened her legs further as she grabbed the back of my head for leverage.

"Take the dress off. I want to see all of you," I told her as I looked up at her. Her face was full of pleasure and I hadn't even licked on her yet. Although she was beautiful as fuck, I needed to see all of her. I wanted to admire the beauty of her in the nude in case this would be my last time witnessing such perfection.

She started to let me go but fell back a little. I grabbed her back, catching her.

"I'll fall," she said, looking down at me.

"Take it off, Storm," I commanded as I firmly held onto her.

Finally, she did what the fuck she was told. Again, I moaned damn as her perfect titties fell from up under the dress. I swear on everything I love, her skin was the finest shade of brown. Perfect, flawless. Bronzed.

My dick pulsated in anticipation. I grabbed hold of her thighs as she placed her hands back on the back of my head. I stuck my tongue completely out and lightly licked on her clit. And then I sat back on the couch, and pulled her pussy closer to my face. With my tongue flat, I rubbed it against her pussy. I spread her puffy pussy lips and buried my face and tongue as far as it allowed me to. I wanted to suck the soul out of her pussy. She tasted just that good. Her pussy juice was sweet, and thick. Her entire vagina was covered in it.

"Ride my face, Storm. Grind ya fucking hips, baby," I told her, as I drunk on her juice like I was dying of thirst.

She grabbed the back of my neck, pushing me further into her pussy. A nigga could barely breathe but I didn't give a fuck. I wanted her pussy to smother me. I wanted it all over my face. Never in my life had I tasted anything more pleasing. My dick was so hard it was staring to hurt.

"Oh my...oh shit," yelled Storm over and over. "Fuck I missed this shit! Yesss, right there baby...mmmm, don't stop!"

I missed it too. Missed her pussy on my face so got damn much. A nigga was going through heavy withdrawals.

I grabbed her hips, and in one motion, I had her sitting on my lap. She didn't sit there long though. As soon as I let her hips go, she jumped up and covered my dick with her full lips. Looking up at a nigga with them sexy ass brown eyes, as she coated my dick with her saliva.

"Damn I taste good," she moaned as she grabbed the base of my dick and stroked me with excitement.

"Sssss. Shit, slow down br-brown skin," I told her with my eyes tightly closed.

"Open your eyes...look...look at me,"

I opened my eyes and she was rubbing the head of my dick on her lips like Chap Stick or some shit. Her lips were so wet. She slowly stroked me as she rubbed it all over her face, never breaking eye contact. I bit on my bottom lip, trying to control the urge to cum. This shit...shit felt to mothafucking good.

I snatched her up and grabbed the back of her neck, pulling her into a deep kiss. I stood up and backed her up against the wall as my dick poked her in the stomach. I wrapped my hands around her neck and she moaned as she rested the back of her head against the wall. I lifted her and slowly slid her down the wall, on my dick.

"Ummm," I said as I entered her whole.

Storm's eyes rolled into the back of head, "Ohhhh. Daaaaamn. So fucking good. Shit!"

She gravitated her hips as I gave her slow strokes. I stared into her eyes and fell in love all over again. She had me in a trance. Had me exactly where she wanted me. In that moment, I didn't give a fuck about the risk. Pussy felt too good to give a fuck about anything other than enjoying the moment. I enjoyed it so much that I never wanted it to end. I wanted to fuck her all day, every day. Wanted the problems of the world to fade into the background.

I just wanted to be with her. Wanted to be connected to her all day, every day. Just. Like. This. Dick buried balls deep, hitting her walls with perfection. The way her pussy hugged a nigga's dick was nothing short of impeccable. Peep how she got a nigga speaking. On some totally different shit.

"Damn...I fucking love you, girl," I told her before going as deep as her pussy would allow me to.

She moaned and gripped my dick with her muscles, "I love you...love you too. So fucking much, Vice. Aahhh, shit you're so deep."

I was making love to her. I didn't want to but I'd be damn! I couldn't help it. She was perfect. Perfect for me. But I wasn't perfect for her. What type of bullshit is that?

Again, I covered her mouth with mine. She softly sucked on my top lip, as I sucked on her bottom on. I grabbed her ass cheeks and opened then so I could get deeper. She locked her legs around me and I pushed her further against the wall.

"I'm cumming—

"Shhh."

I was trying not to bust. Hearing her moan about cumming was going to send me over the fucking edge. Not that it mattered, because as soon as I felt her cum running down my dick, I did just that. I came inside of her. And I didn't give a damn. She didn't neither because she stayed there letting the cum marinate in the pussy.

*

We were laid out on the couch. Storm laid on my chest. I was bugging because once again, our hearts were beating in sync. What the fuck does that mean? If that wasn't enough to make me stay with her then what? But I couldn't. I was about to be on some real fuck nigga shit. She's lying here with a smile on her face, rubbing on my tats. I'm about to wipe the smile right off of her beautiful face and that killed me.

"You feel how our hearts are beating at the same tempo," asked Storm as she looked up at my face. "What's wrong?"

She peeped the look on my face. I wasn't smiling. I was in a trance. Mad because I couldn't have her. Mad because this lifestyle was depriving me of my happiness. As much as I hated that, I had no intentions of stopping. Slanging dope was my first love. I couldn't leave it alone. I needed to, but like I said before, I'm not leaving the game unless it's in a fucking casket.

"A lot," I told her as I ran my fingers though her hair.

She lowered her head, grabbed my hand and kissed my fingers, "I won't let you do this to us."

I pulled my hand away, lifted her off of me and sat up. My eyes stayed on the floor as she rubbed on the nape of my neck. Shit had me stressing. I jerked away from her and said, "Ain't shit popping off between us, aight? I only opened the door because it's freezing out there and you got on that little ass dress."

"Aint shit popping off between us but you just ran all up in my pussy though," she snapped. "That shit was intense. We just made love, Vice!"

I stared her in the eyes, "I don't love you though, Storm. I just wanted some pussy. Cold, hard truth, little girl." I lied straight through my teeth.

I jumped up off the couch and headed to the bathroom. I looked over my shoulder and just as I expected, she was on my heels. I ignored her as she stood in the doorway watching me struggle to piss with a hard dick. My shit was on rock hard. Lil' mama looked damn good in that sweater dress. It hugged ever curve she owned with perfection.

Storm stared at me through the mirror, and I stared back at her. She wasn't crying, but she was visibly pissed off. Her arms were crossed over her chest, arched eyebrows wrinkled, lips pressed tightly together, so much fire in her eyes. I shook my head and dick at the same time. Before pulling my boxer briefs back over my ass. After washing my hands, I tried to leave the bathroom but she blocked me in.

Her nose flared as she spoke, "I don't believe you."

I pushed past her and she stumbled back a little. Hurt a nigga to the core. I hated her for making me treat her like this.

"Get the fuck out, Storm." I said as I stood there, gawking at her as she tried to recover from the stumble.

"Stop, Vice. Please," she cried. "You're literally breaking my heart."

I shrugged, "You're breaking your own heart."

My phone rang and I nonchalantly walked off to my bedroom to answer it. I already knew who it was. I was supposed to be at the hotel picking Laila up an hour ago.

Just as I slid the green phone over, Storm knocked my phone out of my hands.

"Fuck you, Vice!"

I looked at her like she was crazy.

I dragged my hands down my face and let out a loud sigh, "I hate this shit."

She slowly approached me and then wrapped her arms around my body, "Then stop."

"I can't brown skin! Understand that a nigga will die out here if... man, just understand that it'd destroy me if something fucked up happened to you because of my shit," I told her as I tried to pull her arms from around me.

She held onto me tighter, "No! I won't let you do this to us, Vice! You sound stupid as hell! Nothing is going to—

I roughly snatched her arms from around me and said, "And how the fuck you know that? You don't know what the fuck you rapping about, shorty. Ay, get yo stupid ass up out of here."

I was treating her like shit and it was killing me. My fear of losing her was deeper than the love I have for her. That shit popping off with Dawson was my fault! What if brown skin wouldn't have taken control of the situation? God gave her a second chance and she'd rather fuck around with the Devil.

She flinched and backed away as tears poured down her face. I wanted to reach out, grab her and never let her go. The shit pained me to my core. A niggas heart was literally hurting.

Storm nodded and said, "Okay, that's enough," she held her hands up, "Fuck you, alright? I don't deserve this shit, what the hell." And then she walked away.

That magnetic attraction I felt for her was pulling me towards her. I had to close the bedroom door to stop myself from running after her ass. When I heard the front door slam I knew it was a wrap. I fucked up. I was making it easy for another nigga to reap the benefits of being with the beautiful woman I fell in love with.

I had to push her ass in the back of my mind. To be honest, no one was capable of that. When we broke up before, I fucked around with Jos and my mind still stayed on Storm. I wouldn't be complete with anybody but her. How am I going to walk around here with half of my heart fucking missing? A piece of me. Shit, brown skin was damn near all of me. I fell hard for her little sexy ass. Can you imagine how much this fucking a nigga up?

My dick got hard at the thought of the way her pussy felt. My mouth salivated at the thought of the way her pussy tasted. I was probably going to miss that shit the most. Aside from that, I was going to miss her period though. Shorty was a fucking rider. Held me down more than any other female ever had. Thorough ass chick.

I sighed, picked my phone up from the floor and hit Laila back.

7.

STORM

Fuck him. I put the pedal to the metal, heading in the direction of Erotic City. I needed to see my bestie. I was pissed off, ruining my flawless makeup. I couldn't believe he talked to me like that. *'Stop fucking with niggas who don't respect the beauty of you.'* He told me that after he fought Branden back at the hookah lounge. Now I'm about to use his words against his ass. Fuck Vice. He wasn't respecting the beauty of me so I'm not dealing with him anymore.

What I was really tripping on was the fact that he used me. I never thought Vice was capable of being such a fucking asshole. Who was I kidding though? He's a man! I just thought he was different. I can't lie…my heart is broken. I understood that he wanted to break up out of the fear of losing me to the streets, but he didn't have to be so nasty about it. I didn't even recognize him. The way he spoke to me was straight up disrespectful. I just hated myself for thinking going over there dressed sexy and fucking him would make him change his mind. I know just how to get his ass together. Just wait and see. He can be a rude ass all he wants too. I know he wants me just as much as I want him. I just have to give him a little nudge.

Twenty minutes later, I was parking at Erotic City next to Jai's beamer. We've barely talked. Mainly because I was embarrassed. I killed fucking around with that nigga and now I'm single. He dumped me after everything I've done for him. I thought all men wanted that ride or die chick? I was that to the core. I accepted his lifestyle, embraced it even and he shat on me. Why is this the thanks I get? What more do I have to do to prove to him that I don't give a damn about the risk?

After giving myself a ho bath and changing my panties, I hopped out. I was busy looking down at my phone when someone roughly bumped into me. I looked up with a frown on my face and said, "Excuse you, got damn!"

She turned around and frowned, "No, excuse you! If you would've been paying attention you would've saw me coming and moved out of my damn way."

I started to cut deep into her ass until I saw the five other women with her. The last thing I wanted to do was get jumped again. I just shook my head and pushed passed them. I was having a horrible ass night. I needed Jai to hook me up with a strong cup of liq. Hell, I'll probably throw some shots back.

US AGAINST EVERYBODY: A DETROIT LOVE

TALE 3   MISS CANDICE

You gon have to do more than just (say it)
You gon have to do less when you (do it)
Lil mama you know I (show it)
Always want you to (prove it)
You gon have to do more than just (say it)
You gon have to do less when you (do it)
Lil mama you know I (show it)
So you gon need to more than just (prove it)

And you know, you know
And you know, in this foreign car let it go
And you know, you know
And you know, in this foreign car let you know

But I'm not sure that you want me
But I now know
You know I know that this ain't right
Cause you want me cause I got dough
Ever since you walked in inside my foreign, slam my door
You know I know that you been on it
But I been on it, on the low

There was a thick dark brown girl on the stage climbing the pole when I walked in. She was nearly to the ceiling. Men stood at the stage throwing knots of money at her. I knew Jai hated watching that shit. She use to make serious cash when she danced. Bartending paid her well but not nearly as much as stripping.

I headed for the bar after I noticed her leaned over, smiling talking to some man. She didn't know I was coming up here. Like I said, I hadn't even talked to her. But fuck that. I miss her. I needed someone to talk to before I did something crazy like keyed Vice's car or put sugar in his tank.

When she noticed me coming her way, she looked more frightened than surprised. The man she was talking to looked over his shoulder in my direction. I realized he wasn't looking at me when the same woman who pumped into me earlier, hurried over to his side.

I stood at the bar, put my bag on the counter and said, "Wassup bitch?"

Jai smiled and walked over to me, "Hey baby! I missed you. What…um…what you doing up here?"

The man who was sitting at the bar talking to Jai stood up and walked passed. When he said, "Wassup Storm?" A cool chill ran over my body. I looked at him and his bitch and her entourage looked over their shoulders at me with smirks on their faces.

"Who the fuck is that?"

Jai waved me off and said, "A customer. I don't even know his na—

"How is it that he knows mine then?," I defensively asked her.

"Did you forget you fucking with one of the most popular niggas in Detroit," Jai replied with much attitude.

I kept my eyes on them until they left the club. Jai could say he knew me because of Vice all she wanted. I knew better. Her ass was lying. I've known her long enough to recognize when she was lying. I turned my attention back to her and told her I knew she was lying but I didn't want to get into that shit right now.

"Give me the strongest drink you got up in this bitch," I told her.

"Whatever ho, I'm not lying," said Jai before grabbing a glass to make my drink, "What's up? I haven't heard from you. Swear I was starting to feel neglected."

I laughed how she had her bottom lip poked out, being extra.

"I've been going through it," I shook my head, "I didn't want to tell you about what's going on because I was embarrassed. Now I just need my sister."

"Am I going to have to fuck Vice up?," asked Jai with her eyebrow raised.

I giggled as she sat my drink in front of me, "On some real shit, we just might have to. The nigga dumped me."

She dramatically gasped and I ran everything down to her. All she did was shake her head and said how we'd be back together before I know it. I didn't think so though. Vice had never spoken to me that way. I was convinced that he was hell bent on not being with me anymore. And honestly, I can't be mad at him about it. He was trying to protect me from his enemies. I should've respected that. Instead, I didn't give a fuck and was willing to stay by his side no matter who was gunning for him.

I couldn't believe the lengths I was willing to go just for our love. I felt that the shit was solid. I knew I'd never get the type of love I get from him from anyone else. His realness was rare. The nigga treated me like royalty. Why was he doing this to us? I sat there sipping my drink thinking about how much he was hurting me. I couldn't believe it hurt this much. I didn't hurt this much when my ex repeatedly cheated on me. Speaking of my worthless ass ex, why is he standing next to me grinning?

"Wassup Storm," yelled Nico over the music.

Jai turned her face up and assisted another customer.

I gave him the side eye and said, "Not a damn thing."

He held his hands up, "I was just being friendly. You look good."

I could say the same thing about him but I wouldn't. Nico's always been attractive. Tall, cocky, very light skin, with brown eyes, full lips and a sharp goatee and long sideburns. He smelled good too. Damn good. His attractiveness is what kept me going back, and the fact that he knew how to work his not so huge penis. His mouthpiece was nice too. In the past, Nico had a hold on me. Right now though, I couldn't give a damn about him. He was standing there in his designer get up, icy jewelry and Cartier Buff's smiling at me like he was up to no good.

"Thank you, Nico."

He took it upon himself to sit down beside me. I looked over at him like he was crazy.

"What you sipping on? Looks like you need to re-up," he said as he pulled a big bank roll from his pocket.

The nigga was trying to floss. When we were together, he had just landed a job at Chrysler after applying every damn time they posted a job up. I was happy for him. I was happy for us because I thought that meant stability. He ran a good game though. We had plans of moving in together and eventually starting a family. He ended up starting a family, alright, without me.

Jai walked back over and said to Nico, "Nigga fall back, she ain't interested in your chump change," she rolled her eyes, "Weak ass."

Jai hated Nico and the feelings were mutual. When Jai asked me if I needed her to fuck Vice up she meant it. Her love for me was deep. She hated anyone and anything that hurt me. Nico had done a number on me. She came to my condo one day and saw how fucked up I was and tracked him down. She pulled a pocket knife out on him and everything.

I giggled and finished my drink off, "Hit me off with another one sis."

Nico bit his bottom lip and stood up, "Give a hood rat a job she don't know how to act. Hood rat ass bitch."

Jai nearly jumped over the bar. I stood up and held her back. I looked over at Nico and said, "Get the fuck away from here, Nico. I'm not fucking with you! Don't you have a family to get back to?"

He looked at me and his eyes softened, "The baby's not mine. I've been trying to reach out to you, Storm but you changed your number." He grabbed my hand and I pulled away. "Can we at least talk?"

I stood there silent for a couple of seconds. Maybe this is the little nudge Vice needs. Maybe I should string Nico along just to get the attention of Vice?

"I'll call you, aight?"

Jai yelled, "Storm are you fucking ser—

I cut her off and said, "Chill sis."

Nico smiled like he won and walked away after leaning over and kissing me on the cheek. The weak ass nigga thought I was still that stupid woman who constantly forgave him. Little did he know, he was just a pawn in a game I was playing. When he walked off, I made eye contact with Reek. Good! I knew he was going to go back and tell Vice everything. I didn't even know he was here but I'm glad he is.

I sat back down and Jai started to grill me. I put my hand up and told her I had a plan. She told me I was playing with fire, looking to be burned. She swore up and down she knew Vice better than I did just because she knew him longer. Jai kept going on and on about how Vice wasn't the type of man to play with. She didn't know him better though. I know all sides of him. I know he's crazy. I just didn't care. I needed him to get his damn mind right.

*

After leaving the club, I headed home. I was drunk as hell but drove anyway. Taking my mind off of Vice was a success. I even tipped a few dancers and talked to a couple of men. I wasn't interested. I just did it because Reek kept watching me. I found it funny and couldn't wait until the morning. I just knew I was going to wake up to a bunch of text messages. Hell, he'll probably pop up on me. Vice hated the idea of anybody else being with me. The news is going to infuriate him.

I hopped out of the car and staggered to the front door.

"You know you shouldn't be driving like that, Storm."

I dropped my keys as I tried to unlock my door. What the fuck was he doing here?

"Did you follow me," I yelled.

"I know where you live, Storm. Why you acting brand new," said Nico leaned up against my house smiling.

"Well, you gotta go!"

He licked his lips and inched in closer to me, "I thought you wanted to talk."

I rolled my eyes, "Over the phone—

"Didn't she tell you to get the fuck on?!"

I looked over my shoulder at Reek and said, "You…what are you doing here?"

Reek walked up on the porch and treaded towards Nico who held his hands up.

"Bro told me to keep an eye out on your drunk ass," he said as he shook his head full of dreads.

I should've been more observant considering the fact that I was kidnapped not even a month ago. I was drunk though. The only thing I was worried about was getting home safely and soaking in the tub.

I smiled, "He did?"

I was totally oblivious to the fact that I was in danger. If I would've been sober I would've noticed the menacing look in Nico's eyes. He wasn't here to talk. The nigga was here to fuck and I'm sure he wouldn't have taken no for an answer. I was on some stupid shit. Out here wearing a skimpy sweater dress, drunk, and playing with his feelings like there was actually a chance of us reconnecting. I had to do better. That shit that happened with Joslyn and Dawson should've taught me to do better. Why was I out here at two in the morning, drunk?

Nico said, "I didn't know you were seeing anybody, S—

"Don't matter my nigga, walk off," Reek said as he stood there with his arms crossed over his shoulder.

"Just go Nico, I'll cal—

"No she won't," Reek told him with a laugh. "Walk off, my dude."

I rolled my eyes and unlocked the door. Nico walked off after telling me good night. I stepped in the house and immediately took my fringe boots off. Reek stood in the doorway until Nico drove off. I sat my bag on the coffee table and asked Reek where Vice was. He told me Vice was busy and told me to have a good night.

I was too drunk to do anything but fall on the couch and pass out.

*

"You really don't give a damn huh?"

I jumped up out of my sleep, clinching my chest. When I opened my eyes, I rolled them into the back of my head.

US AGAINST EVERYBODY: A DETROIT LOVE
TALE 3   MISS CANDICE

"How did you get in my house?"

"This might be your house and the rent might be paid up on it but let's not forget how you got this nice ass condo in the suburbs, Stormy," said Mack.

I sat up and placed my hand on my forehead. It was banging. I could barely remember anything from the night before. I seriously don't even know how I got home.

"That still doesn't explain how you got in, Mack."

He pressed his lips tightly together before saying, "Dad."

I waved him off and stood up off the couch, stretching.

"Oh, fuck! What time is it," I yelled totally disregarding the fact that he is my dad.

I had to work at ten. I grabbed my purse off of the coffee table and rummaged through it until I found my phone. Mack was in my ear about leaving the door unlocked and how I was 'misbehaving'. Is he out of his mind? I'm a grown ass woman. How in the hell am I misbehaving? I still wasn't speaking to him so I didn't respond to anything he said.

I unlocked my phone and shook my head. *9:15AM.* There was no way in hell I was going to make it to work in time. Not with this lethal hang over. I hated to have to call off on Carla but there was nothing more I could do. I should've known better drinking like that on a work night. Vice had me in my feelings though. I couldn't help but need a drink. He had me fucked up. I dragged my notification menu, expecting to see a text from him but it was Carla and Jai. That hurt my feelings. I didn't remember much of what happened last night but I do recall seeing Reek there. I knew I'd have some slick talking text message from Vice after his boy wired him up about me speaking to another man. But nope, there was nothing.

And that frightened me more than Mack who was gawking down at me running his mouth.

"What do you really want? Swear I haven't hear—

Mack interrupted me, "I'm sick of this shit, Storm! You will respect and forgive me. You sholl didn't hesitate to forgive the nigga responsible for your kidnapping did you? You speaking to that weak ass ni—"

I cut him off, "Really? I mean…REALLY? Is this what you want to do Mack?"

He lowered his head, "I just want my princess to forgive me, alright?"

"Oh, I forgive you but that's it. What you thought? I'd just dust you putting me in danger under the rug? You've got it twisted."

"And Vice didn't? You could've died!"

"You might as well stop comparing the situations! The difference is, Vice didn't send people to shoot up a spot I was at! No! What happened was totally different. You need to go!"

He loudly sighed, "This shit is eating me up, Stormy. I fucked up alright," he grabbed my hand and said, "What happened with your kidnapping scared the shit out of me. All time is precious, baby girl. Holding grudges ain't good."

I sat there, on top of my coffee table, lips turned and twisted up. I didn't give a got damn about it eating him up. It should be. Our relationship will never be the same.

"What do you want me to do?"

"Let's go on a date, sweetie. The movies and skating. Remember how much you liked ska—

"When I was a kid," I replied in disgust. I took my hand away and stood up. "I have stuff to do. I'll call you."

135

Mack was torn up and I really didn't care. I could've been killed! I know you're supposed to honor and respect your parents but that nigga didn't deserve neither. He nodded and turned to leave. Before he walked out he told me he loved me. I told him I loved him too. Of course I love the nigga. He's my dad. I just can't stand his reckless, disrespectful old ass. He smiled and walked out. He thought there was hope but nope, there isn't any. I'm not calling him, so I'm definitely not going on a date with him.

I called Carla and told her about what happened last night. She wasn't happy about me calling off since this was our busiest time of year. Christmas was right around the corner. I told her I'd be no good if I came in. And I wasn't lying. I knew shit was real when I had my face in the toilet bowl, throwing up.

Hours later, I was still in the same shape. But I was worst. I spent all of my time in bed, on Facebook, Instagram, and Twitter. I was trying my hardest not to call Vice. I missed him so much and couldn't believe he hadn't called me. What happened last night was slowly but surely coming back to me. I remembered Reek following me home and basically saving me from Nico. So why hadn't Vice called me? I mean damn, it's that serious?

I felt nauseous and sat up. I grabbed the bucket next to my bed. I held my stomach as I leaned over and puked inside of the bucket. I was sick as hell. My phone notification went off and I grabbed it. When I pulled the menu down I almost passed out.

My period is two weeks late. How in the hell did I miss that?

8.

JAI

I rolled my eyes as I sat my phone back on the nightstand. Tech's ass was beginning to be a problem. There were many times when I wanted to hit Vice up and tell him everything. But the way Tech threatened me had a bitch shaking in her boots. Vice is nutty, but I think Tech is a fucking psychopath. Besides, Vice will never know I was responsible for what Tech has planned for him. I just hope Vice is smart enough not to fall for the shit.

I grabbed my phone and finally texted Tech back.

Me: (4:43PM) I told you everything. Now leave me tf alone.

Tech was trying to get me to tell him more about Storm. I wouldn't. All I gave him was her name and that was fucked up. I was not going to put my friend in danger. His crazy ass wanted to know where she worked and lived. Is he retarded? I swear, I want to kill his ass myself. I love Storm with my whole heart. She's been through enough and I'd never do anything like that to her. Vice is a totally different story. Fuck Vice when it comes to me living. Now, if something happened to Storm behind me running my mouth I'll fucking die myself.

I yawned and sat up. It was damn near five in the evening. My ass was burned out! Thank God I'm not working tonight. Instead, I plan on visiting Ryan. Yeah, the nigga is still heavy on my mind. We don't talk anymore and that's really been bothering me. I have new friends but they don't compare to Ryan's ugly ass. It's obvious they all have hidden agendas but bitch I do too so I couldn't care less. I wasn't expecting anything but paper from them anyway.

After showering and making sure I was on my bad bitch shit, I hopped in the car and headed for Michigan State University. I had a long ride ahead of me but I didn't give a damn. Ryan wasn't going to speak to me over the phone. He wasn't going to have much of anything to say to me in person but I have my ways of persuasion.

*

Finally, after an hour and thirty minutes, I was pulling up in front of the campus. It was cold out but I was bundled up and ready to walk around campus until I found him. I was on some other shit but I just didn't care. I wanted some explanation. I needed to know who the girl and baby was. He claimed it wasn't his and by the looks of Facebook he never claimed him.

I've been snooping my ass off. I had to stop myself from commenting on the girls status about Ryan being a no good nigga. She was describing a total stranger to me. I knew Ryan didn't get down how she was claiming he did. All of her little friends and family were talking shit about him too. Her current boyfriend was even running his mouth saying how he would take care of JR. Yes, bitch, the baby is a junior. But, if Ryan says he's not his then I should believe him right? I don't fucking know. All I do know is, I missed him like crazy.

I wrapped my infinity fringe scarf tighter around my neck, and buttoned the top button of my double-breasted peplum pea coat before shutting the engine off. All eyes were on me. I was pushing a pink fucking Benz, of course they were watching. I wished I could've been a lot more incognito. I've given putting this car up until the summer much though. But it's become my favorite. I guess I would have to pull the Challenger back out. This was a time I didn't want all eyes on me.

I got out the car and began my search. I was tempted to ask people if they knew him. I ended up not needing to. I found his ass standing outside of one of the buildings, smiling, talking to some girl. I was caught by surprise because the girl was cute. A very cute dark skin girl with faux locs.

I stuffed my hands in my pockets and put on my baddest catwalk as I treaded towards them. The girl gave Ryan a hug and walked away. When he turned around and saw me coming his way he frowned up. I smiled and yelled, "Who was that, Ryan?"

The girl was still in hearing distant. She looked over her shoulder with wrinkled eyebrows. But she didn't come over. I wanted her too. I needed me a reason to beat the hell out of someone. I was furious because he was occupying his time with someone else.

"What you doing up here," asked Ryan as he adjusted his backpack on his shoulder.

"We need to talk," I glanced at the girl who stopped walking. "I asked you a question."

"My fucking classmate, Jai. Not that it's any of your business." Said Ryan as he looked over his shoulder at the girl. He nodded at her and she walked away. What the hell was that?

"And what was tha—

Ryan grabbed my arm and we walked off, "She was making sure I was good. Do you think if it was more than what I said that she would've walked away? Be serious, Jai."

I yanked away and wiped my nose with the back of my gloved hand, "Its cold out here. Can we talk someplace?"

"In your whip. Because as soon as we're done, you're leaving."

My stomach dropped and I nodded. He was hurting me and I hated it.

When we finally got into my car, I turned started the engine and cut the heat on full blast. I snatched my gloves off and blew into my hands. Ryan sat there watching me the entire time. Well, not me. He was looking at my tattoo. I rolled my eyes and placed my hands in between my thighs. Ryan turned away and looked out of the window while shaking his head.

"What did you drive all the way up here for, shawty?" Asked Ryan without giving me any eye contact.

"Us."

He turned my way and said, "Ain't no us."

I sighed and told him, "that's because you think I have ulterior motives."

"And am I wrong? You tryna break a nigga."

Again, I explained to him how I got the tattoo when I was younger. I also kept it real about how I did have intentions of using him for money in the beginning. He asked me why he should believe I still don't have those intentions. It took me a minute but I finally confessed to loving him. Got damn a bitch didn't want to utter that damn word. I've been ignoring the fact that I only cared so much because I loved him. I've never loved any man. This was different for me. Ryan tensed up and sighed.

"Do you love me, Ryan?" I boldly asked him like I wasn't a nervous wreck.

"What you think?"

I smiled a little. He loved me. He was just afraid of actually admitting it because of my past. I told him I wasn't on that bull shit anymore. He still didn't believe me.

"You're having a hard time believing me because of 'what's her name'." I told him with my lips twisted up.

I couldn't wait to bring her up. I needed to get down to the bottom of everything. Ryan didn't say anything so I kept at it. I asked him what was up with her. He explained to me how he was going through some legal things. She wouldn't respond to the paternity testing but kept on claiming how Ryan's the dad. Ryan told me Keisha only planted the baby on him because she's a gold digger. She found out about all of the NFL offers Ryan had lined out and saw dollar signs. He was extremely stressed out about the ordeal. That's why when I called him he was so rude.

"I apologize about all of that, shawty." Said Ryan with his hand on my thigh. "What she's doing is tarnishing my name."

"It shouldn't even matter. It's obvious that the baby isn't yours since she won't even agree to the testing."

Ryan nodded and scratched his chin, "True. I've got some good news though."

I smiled while he told me about how he would be playing for the Patriots next season. Bitch, you know I saw dollar signs but that's not all though. I really didn't have any gold digging intentions with this. I was simply happy for him.

"I do love you, Jai but it's going to take me a long time to trust you." Ryan told me as he looked into my eyes.

I understood so I nodded my head.

"Are we friends again?" I asked with puppy dog eyes.

He playfully mushed me in the head, "More than friends, shawty."

I leaned over and kissed him on the lips. A first for me. A small jester that'd show him how serious I was.

*

TALE 3   MISS CANDICE

"Bitch, you can keep ignoring me if you want to." Yelled Tech into the phone.

I pulled it away from my ear, as I sped down the freeway.

"I'm not ignoring your ass Tech! What do you wa—

"You know what the fuck I want. Lace me up with that info Jai."

"I can't give you that."

"You want to die?"

No I didn't want to die. But I didn't want my friend to neither. My palms sweated as I gripped the steering wheel. Tears welled up into my eyes as I thought about what I was getting ready to do. I was stuck between a rock and a hard place. I was finally in a happy place with Ryan but like a thief in the night, Tech had called me and snatched that happiness right away. Why was I caught in the middle of this shit?

"No I don't want to die, Tech. Aight? I mean damn! You're cooking up a scheme to get him. Why do my friend have to be caught in the middle?"

"Because I want that nigga hurt in more ways than one."

And then a light bulb went off in my head. Storm told me Vice had a sister he just reconnected with.

"He has a sister." I told him in hopes of him showing interest in her instead.

But he didn't. "Fuck her. I want Storm."

"They not even toge—

"Don't give a fuck about that neither."

I silently cried as I gave him the information he wanted.

9.

REEK

"Am I gon' have to mask up, bro?" I asked Vice when he pulled up in front of the crib.

We were on a mission. One of our houses were hit and my nigga knew who was behind it. Some dirty niggas from around the way. I couldn't understand for the life of me why these stupid fucks kept trying us. You'd think they would be making better decisions by now. Young bums got away with a few kilos, some weed, and a case of promethazine. I'm usually a laid back cat, but this shit here... this shit had to be handled in the worst way. Bro was on some buck shit, and ready to dead whoever stood in the way. He was already spazzing because of the shit going on with him and Storm. Not only that, but Detective Thompson was back to rearing her ugly head. Ain't no telling what this nigga had in mind.

"Fuck no! I want these pussies and whoever in the crib to get a good look at me." Said Vice as he loaded the two burners in his lap. "I'm about to roll up in there on some militant shit, brodie!"

147

I nodded and opened the passenger door to hop in. Bro said militant and I'm always strapped and ready for war. I put my seat belt on 'cause I knew this nigga was about to do about seventy on the mile. Vice was dumb heated. Whatever these fuck boys had coming to them was their faults. I couldn't wait to spill blood off the strength of principles alone. Fuck they thought they were dealing with? Some lame niggas? Man nah, everybody in the hood knew how he got down. But see…these were some eight mile ass niggas.

"You think somebody sent them niggas?," I asked Vice as I held onto the door. Nigga was running lights and everything. I had to tell him to cool it. He wasn't hearing me though. He didn't even respond to my question.

I just pulled the glock from my waistband and sat it in my lap.

When we pulled up in front of the house, two lil niggas walked inside. Looked to be about ten and eleven. When bro snatched the door open, I knew he no longer gave a fuck about his no kid rule. We didn't let off shots in the presence of kids. He didn't give a fuck now, and neither did I. This shit had to be dealt with pronto.

It was dark out, and we wore all black on some true ass sniper shit. Thing is though, we were hitting these niggas in plain view. Fuck shooting for a distant. I wanted to get some blood on me. I wanted to watch a nigga's melon split wide open. We crotched down as we walked up on the porch. Future's Codeine Crazy was blasting when we barged in.

Pour that bubble in,
Drink that muddy drink
That muddy drink that muddy when we're cuddling
Yeah I'm covered in
I was thugging it
I was just loving it
That's for them other niggas
That's for them other bitches
They ain't for you dog
That's for them other niggas
That ain't for you shorty
That's for the other bitches
I'm going crazy bout it
I'm going codeine crazy
That's how I'm living it
I'm feeling lovely
I'm drinking bubbly
I'm drinking bubbly

These niggas were sprawled out on the couch, fucked up! Every last one of them. The music was blasting so they didn't hear when we barged in. I kicked an empty box, that once held over ten bottles of promethazine. I turned to Vice shaking my head. He motioned for me to hit the back of the house to find the two younger cats that walked in before we did. I kept my gun up as I slowly walked to the back of the house. I heard rumbling behind a closed door. Before I kicked the door down, I looked over my shoulder to see if bro was straight. He was smooth, gun up, eyes on the four niggas on the couch making sure they didn't wake up.

I kicked the door down and the two niggas jumped back. Both of them had white powder on their noses. I waved the pistol in their faces and they screamed and held their hands up. Next thing I knew, the music stopped and I heard a loud crashing noise and a single shot ring off. I knew Vice was putting in work.

"Get out. Take y'all young asses to the living room. Come learn something, dummies." I told them as they backed out of the bathroom.

When we made it to the living room, I couldn't believe my fucking eyes. Vice had them niggas stripped down to their boxer, on their knees with their hands up. One of the niggas had a plastic grocery bag over his head, struggling to breathe while Vice talked his shit.

"Fuck is wrong with you bum niggas?!" he yelled as he held onto the grocery bag. "Nobody told y'all about Vice huh?!" He laughed, "I'm the mothafucking Grim reaper, pussies! I do this killing shit for fun! I send niggas to the Lord for fun! I was waiting on a nigga to act up. Itching to murk me a stupid nigga!"

"Shawn…what's… what's going on?" yelled the chubby one of the kids I found in the bathroom snorting.

"Peewee? Man, what you doing in here?" said one of the niggas in his underwear.

"Please don't kill my big brother." Cried Peewee.

Vice looked up and said, "Nigga, fuck your big brother." He pointed his gun at Shawn and sent a bullet in between his eyes.

Peewee fell to the floor and cried. I felt sympathy for the lil nigga. He didn't look to be no older than twelve and he just witnessed his brother get killed. That shit was going to eat at him for the rest of his life. He probably looked up to the pussy nigga, too. You know how it is. See yo big brother out here making moves, doing shit…and you want to be just like him. Shawn probably was the niggas hero. He shouldn't have been but you know how it go.

The other young cat I caught snorting, tried to run away and Vice hit him in the face with the butt of his gun. The stupid niggas who robbed us moaned and

151

groaned about how Vice wasn't right. The dude with his head in the grocery bag stopped fighting for air, and Vice let the bag go. He fell to the floor, dead. I shook my head at how shit was going down. My nigga ain't never been this reckless.

"Ay bro, you ready to dip?"

Vice looked up at me, his hazel eyes glossed over with coldness.

"In a minute nigga!" he yelled before putting a bullet in the remaining niggas head. "I'm ready now."

I shook my head and looked down at Peewee and over at his friend, "What we gone do with these lil dudes?"

Vice shrugged his shoulders and said, "Leave 'em." He looked over at Peewee, "Ay my mans, if you feel some type of animosity in your heart for me in say…six, seven years…come see me. I'm always ready for gun play."

Peewee didn't say anything as he crawled over to his brother. I just kept shaking my head. Vice is a motherfucking animal, yo. No lie. No remorse.

*

After we got what was left of our shit out of the house, we left. Peewee and his friend stayed there sobbing over the loss of their families. The shit ate at me as we made our way back to seven mile in silence. This is why I don't kill in front of kids. The shit is fucked up. Them stupid cats needed to be dealt with but I really regret doing it in front of the young cats. They didn't need to see that shit.

I glanced at Vice and he was bobbing his head to Blade Icewood, Ride on Me.

"I heard they wanna ride on me! Bitch nigga bring it on! Got the Chrome on my lap as we speak! I heard they wanna ride on me! Nigga, I ain't never scared! I'm at the club every night, I'm everywhere!" He yelled, hype as hell bouncing in his seat.

He was on one. Spazzing. Feeling untouchable like that nigga Blade, a rapper and Detroit celebrity, felt before he was killed. I looked at my bro hopping he wouldn't soon meet his maker.

"You hear this shit that nigga Blade spitting Reek!? Niggas always trying me yo! Why niggas gotta try me, bro?! Huh? Knowing I don't give a fuck. A nigga rreeeeally must be on some don't give a fuck shit nowadays. Can you believe I split that boy wig in front of his lil' bro?," Vice yelled over the music with a smile on his face. "Fuck 'em! Fuck rules! Shit gets in the way my nigga. I don't have time to be chasing fuck boys all around the city just to send a hot one through 'em. That shit had to be handled regardless! Vice is a test niggas will always fail. I thought they found that out years ago."

I didn't say anything. I just laid my head back on the headrest and closed my eyes.

10.

VICE

It was obvious that the nigga Reek was feeling some type of way. I couldn't wait to get the pussy up out of my whip. I couldn't give a fuck less about him having ill feelings about me murking ol boy off in front of his little brother. For one, in my eyes, the lil nigga was a grown ass man. He was posted up in the trap with a group of bum ass thieves. Not to mention, his 'grown' ass had coke dust on his nose. MY mothafucking coke dust. Them young boys better be happy I didn't send a bullet ripping through their domes, too, for snorting my shit. As a matter of fact, I just might swing back around there in a couple of day to do just that.

Rules didn't matter to me anymore. Boundaries and shit went out the window when my own flesh and blood switched up on me. And when a broad I thought was riding with me right or wrong, fucking with her or not, switched up on me. Nobody was safe. Not a soul on this earth is exempt from me. Anybody can eat these bullets. Fuck 'em. If you ain't with me, then mothafucka, you're against me. And anybody who knows me, know that's the wrong side to be on.

My phone rang and I looked at the screen. Brown skin had been hitting me up all night. I never picked up though, straight up sent my lil' baby to voicemail. I needed her bad as fuck right now. The mood I was in was so vicious, the shit scared me a little. But despite needing to feel her lil' body up against mine, I knew it was best for me to keep my distance although it was hard as fuck.

I pulled away from the gas station after lighting the fat blunt I just rolled a minute ago. A lot had transpired over the past twenty-four hours. Last night was very eventful. If it wasn't for the crazy shit I got myself into, I would've been the one trailing brown skin's reckless ass home. Thank God my right hand was on it. Ain't no telling what type of shit her pussy ass ex would've tried to pull. Lil' mama had to do better.

After having dinner with Laila, I took her back to the hotel. She explained to me how she was sick and tired of staying in the hotel. She missed home and was ready to go back. Thing is, home was where the fuck nigga who put hands on her stayed. I nipped that shit in the bud so quick. I told her I'd find her a house today. And like always, I delivered. Sis was situated in a nice lil ranch out in Warren, off of Martin road and twelve mile.

Coping her a crib raised some questions. She asked me how I made money. She took notice of the lavish life I lived and not once did I mention a job. I told her suspect ass I gambled for a living and was damn good at it. Fuck I look like keeping it all the way G with her? I didn't know her, yo. We're totally different people now. Hell, knowing a person don't even matter these days. Anybody is liable to flip shit on you. Besides, Laila seemed really guarded, like she was hiding something from me. Thing is, her nervousness could've been behind the fact that she was getting the fuck beat out of her. Either way, I planned on doing some digging. I just needed me a reliable source, and a gullible bitch to lay pipe to. Nothing is off limits when you have a bitch high off dick.

I turned my stereo up and zoned out as I headed in the direction of home. A nigga was dead ass tired. After putting in mad work, and dropping the drugs back off at the crib I wanted nothing more than to hit the bed. I wished like hell I could be riding home to brown skin. I needed her like, mad crazy. The problems of the world faded into the background when I was in her presence. The smell of her gave me a high I couldn't describe. The type of high I couldn't acquire from blowing L's or sipping.

As Man in The mirror, a track off of Jadakiss's new album blasted from the speakers, I couldn't help but relate to the lyrics.

I'm on a paper chase, they want me out of my zone.

Spread the product, get the profit, I'm gone.

Yeah, high as fuck, driving alone.

Spread the product, get the profit, I'm gone.

Sometimes I can feel the hate when it's nearest

I can see it clearer than the man in the mirror (yeah)

Feeling down and I'm telling myself cheer up

I'm only scared of God and the man in the mirror.

The shit that transpired tonight was all the confirmation I needed. I've always been a loose cannon but now, I felt myself slipping over to a darker side. Sometimes I felt like I didn't even fear God. I felt untouchable, without a fearing bone in my body. The only person I truly feared was myself; the man in the mirror. I didn't know what type of shit I was capable of doing. Sometimes I shocked myself. I was pissed off with nothing to ease the anger. No pretty lil' brown skin to soothe me. No Storm to rub my back and tell me she loved me. She's my favorite place to go when I needed peace. Without that balance, I was turning into a scary nigga. With no boundaries... no lines to be crossed. Nothing was undoable. Nothing was off limits. A nigga's granny could get it. I just didn't give a fuck anymore.

I looked in the rearview mirror at the flashing red and blue lights behind me. This bitch. I put the blunt out and pulled over. I watched her strutting over to my car with her badge dangling from her neck. I'm sick and tired of this bitch. I reached for the banger underneath my seat and stopped myself. What the fuck was I thinking? The unmarked car she was riding in definitely had cameras attached to it. I was trying to send myself under the fucking jail. I kicked the gun further under the seat just as she tapped on my window.

I let it down and smoke hit her in the face. I didn't give a flying fuck.

"You must really want this beef, huh, Olivia?" I asked her with a smirk on my face.

She fanned the smoke out of her face and choked a little. Then she leaned into my window with her titties spilling all out of her trench coat.

"You know, I can lock your arrogant ass up for possession of marijuana right—

I cut her off and held my hands up, twisting my wrist in her face, "do what you must, my baby."

"—But I'd rather take you down for a more serious charge. I'm thinking, quadruple homicide?" she smiled, "What do you think?"

"I think your lonely, overworked and underpaid ass want this beef doe, on the real. Otherwise, why would you be following me at two in the morning by yourself," I asked, clearly unfazed by her trying to pin that murder on me. Obviously, the bitch didn't have any evidence.

"Quadruple homicide, Vice. Do you know how much time that is?," she giggled, her titties bouncing as she laughed.

I made my staring obvious. I was letting the stupid bitch know I couldn't care less about the homicide she was talking about. Like I said, if she had evidence this shit would be going totally different. I licked my lips and looked up her, causing her to stop talking midsentence. She was talking shit about me finally being locked up. She kept going on and on about how she was happy to be finally ridding the city of scum like me. But when the bitch laid eyes on these dreamy ass hazel eyes, captivating her like I did every broad I've ever wanted, she shut up.

"What was that, Detective?" I asked, as I never broke eye contact.

Detective Olivia Thompson is a nice looking broad. 5'7, Caramel colored, big brown eyes, sandy brown hair, big lips, curvy but petite, with just enough ass, her titties were big as hell, and gap-toothed. Not the prettiest, but I wasn't trying to do anything but get my nuts drained. When she was first assigned to my case, none of this shit would be possible. I think laying eyes on this monster in my pants a few months ago, flipped shit. She was hanging around more and making sly remarks. Yeah, Detective wanted this beef!

TALE 3   MISS CANDICE

"Um... out... out of the car," she yelled as she backed away, with her hand on the pistol attached to her belt. Although she was in plain clothes, she wore her duty belt.

Bitch wanted to get her feels on. That's cool too. I'm going to make sure this dick extra hard for her too. My mind instantly went to Storm and how sexy she was. I thought about how good her pussy tasted. My dick stood at attention almost immediately. My hard on was going to be hella visible in these black Nike joggers.

I hopped out the car, and as expected her eyes landed right on my dick. I smirked and said, "Wassup Olivia?" I held my arms up as she began to frisk me. She lightly brushed up against my dick, and I made it jump. "That's the only weapon I'm concealing, my baby. A weapon of mass destruction."

I heard her groan and she brushed up against it again. I dropped my arms and grabbed her wrist, then pulled her closer to my chest. She looked up at me, panting heavily.

"Let me go," Detective Thompson moaned.

My dick was positioned right on her pussy. I pulled her closer, "You don't want me to though. You want this dick, don't you?" She didn't say anything and I repeated my question.

"Let me go," she moaned again.

"Not until you admit to wanting to fuck me, Detective."

She looked away and then back at me. If she really wanted to get away from me, she could've snatched her wrist free. I wasn't even holding her tight.

"I...yes, Vice but that means no—

I let her go and pinned her up against my car with her arms over her head. We were in a secluded area with nothing but an abandoned warehouse to the left of us. The grass was high, and the one streetlight kept flickering on and off.

I kissed her on the neck and whispered in her ear, "You want me to provide you with it, my baby?"

She moaned and wrapped her long legs around me, "In...in the car."

I snatched the door open and got inside. With her on my lap, aggressively kissing and rubbing on me, I reclined the seat. I pulled the baton from her belt and ran it across her full breast, and then over her pussy. I lightly tapped on it and she moaned.

"Oh my God, what am I doing?," moaned Detective Olivia.

US AGAINST EVERYBODY: A DETROIT LOVE

TALE 3   MISS CANDICE

"Rewarding yourself with this good dick," I told her as I snatched her trench coat open. She moaned and her titties fell freely in my face. Bitch didn't even have on a shirt or bra. Nasty ho probably took them off before she pulled me over. She knew what she wanted before I even presented her with the offer.

That there told me that Olivia would do whatever I wanted her to. Simply because this idea wasn't mine – it was hers which meant she was willing to risk losing her job. Good. I'm going to put this bitch to work and then get rid of her. I threw her baton in the passenger seat and wrapped my hands around her neck as I roughly sucked on her nipples. She moaned and told me to choke harder. I gave her what she wanted.

She hungrily pulled my dick from my joggers – I was out here free balling; no boxers. She leaned down and wrapped her big ass lips around my dick. She stroked me as her thick saliva coated my dick. I grabbed a fist full of her hair and slammed her head down on my dick. I was angry fucking this bitch. I didn't want anything to do with her. But I needed her for information on Laila. Usually, I'd be able to get information from people in the hood but this was different. Laila didn't know anybody in the hood. She was hard to dig up info on. So here I am, fucking with this pig ass bitch.

I wanted nothing more than to be fucking with Storm right now. I closed my eyes and imagined that it was her giving me dome instead of this bitch. I can't though, Olivia could suck a mean dick.

She cupped my balls and sucked on them while stroking my dick.

"Off the balls, and back on that meat bitch," I told her as I roughly snatched her head away from my balls.

"Yes, daddy," she moaned. Bitch was liking this. She didn't mind my roughness at all.

I thrusted my hips in her face, pushing my massive dick to the back of her throat. She gagged and spit a big glob of spit on my dick before going back to work. This had to be the wettest, sloppiest head I've ever gotten. I was enjoying the shit. She placed her hands on my thighs and eased her mouth onto my dick, taking me all in inch my inch.

"Fuck," I groaned.

And then her lips tightened around me as she went up and down. She grabbed onto the base of my dick and moved her hands in a twisting motion as she stroke me. I pulled her head away when I felt myself on the verge of cumming.

I grabbed a Magnum from my middle console and slid it on before saying, "Hop on this dick, freak." I paused, "Matter of fact, turn around."

US AGAINST EVERYBODY: A DETROIT LOVE

TALE 3   MISS CANDICE

She turned around and I grabbed her handcuffs from her belt before she pulled her jeans down. I grabbed her wrist and cuffed her to the steering wheel before sliding into her pussy. She was wet and tight as fuck like a virgin. I could barely move around.

"Ohhh... oowwww," she screamed.

I didn't care about the obvious discomfort she was in, and went to wrecking that pussy. I grabbed her hips and went as deep as her tight hole would let me. She cried out about how good it felt when I pinched on her swollen clit. The entire time I fucked her, I thought of Storm. Shorty had me under a spell. Olivia's pussy felt good but it wasn't as good as brown skins. When Olivia looked over her shoulder at me, I placed Storm's face on hers. So fucking pretty.

When I moved my hips in a circular motion, I felt her juices wetting my thighs up. Bitch was wet as hell. I slowly pulled out of her, and then forcefully reentered her. She let out the loudest moan to ever fill my ears. Yeah, this bitch been wanting the dick. She was too turned on.

I uncuffed her and told her to bounce on my dick. She was a little reluctant but did so anyway. When she wouldn't move like I wanted her too, I grabbed her hips and moved her back and forth me as I dug my dick deeper within her walls. I reached up and played with her pierced nipples. Freak thot bitch.

"You like this shit don't you?" I whispered in her ear as I gave her long strokes.

"Yessss. I love it." She moaned.

"You my bitch now, right?" I asked as I pinched her nipples.

"Mmhmm, damn this is good," she said as she threw her head back on my shoulder.

I grabbed her neck and bit on the side of her face, "You gone do whatever the fuck I tell u to do right?"

She didn't respond, so I roughly smacked on her clit with my freehand and repeated the question.

Olivia let out another loud moan before trying to close her legs. I roughly pulled them apart and kept tapping on her clit.

"Answer me, detective," I lowly said in her ear.

"Mmhm, yes, whateverrrr."

I grabbed the baton off the seat and shoved it into her mouth. She sucked on it like it was a dick. Dirty bitch. I tightly closed my eyes as I rammed in and out of her. Her pussy muscles clamped down on my dick. Her juices were so thick, and her smell so potent. She didn't stink or anything. Just smelled just like pussy. I shoved the baton further down her throat and she gagged. I removed it and rubbed on her pussy with it. She was in my ear about how good it felt. When she told me she was about to cum, I dug deeper.

"I can feel it in my chessst. Oh my fucking goodness," she cried out.

I grunted and released inside of the condom. She climbed off of me and plopped down on the passenger seat. I looked down at the condom and it was lightly coated with blood.

"Bitch, did you just come on your period?"

Olivia's light cheeks turned pink, "No... I haven't had sex in years. Not to mention, your dick is humongous."

I snatched it off and tossed it out of the window.

*

The next morning I woke up feeling guilty as hell. Brown skin might not be my girl anymore but the way I've been treating her was eating me up. I grabbed my phone from the nightstand just as someone banged on my front door. I sat the phone down and wiped crust from my eyes. I grabbed my gun from the pillow next to me and got out of bed.

"Fuck is it," I yelled.

I looked through the peephole and it was Storm. She had bags under her eyes, and she was dressed in PINK pajamas and UGG boots. I sat the gun on the table and opened up. Her arms were crossed over her chest.

"Wass—

She pushed past me and walked into the house, "You can't answer your fucking phone?"

I shut the door behind her and stood there rubbing my eyes, "I told you—

She tossed something at my feet and I bent down to pick it up. It was a pregnancy test with two pink lines on it. My heart sped up and I looked up at her. She was frowned up with her lips poking out.

"You're pregnant?"

Storm looked away and wiped a tear from her eyes with the sleeve of her North Face coat, "Unfortunately."

I stared down at the stick as I walked over to the couch. A shorty? A fucking kid? The timing was screwed up but I was happy. I looked over at her standing by the door and held my arms open. She rolled her eyes but she walked her ass over to me. I pulled her down on my lap and kissed her on the forehead.

"The timing is unfortunate but the pregnancy definitely isn't," I told her as I looked down into her eyes. "Stop crying Storm, we're going to figure this shit out."

I said I wasn't leaving the game unless it was in a casket. Not once did a child cross my mind. No way in fuck was I going to bring a child in this world on the tip I was on now. I had possibly nine months to wrap shit up.

11.

STORM

"Now you'll have me huh," I asked him as I wiped snot from my nose with a napkin from my pocket.

"Of course. Things have changed, you kno—

"I've been thinking about an abortion. If a baby is the only thing that'll allow us to be toget—

"Don't ever utter the word abortion to me," said Vice as he held me tighter. "Stop bugging. What I meant by things changed was that now I need to protect you in a different way. Pushing you away was all fine and dandy before my seed got thrown into the equation. I have to wrap shit up and pull out."

I laughed, "Vice, you'll never leave the game."

He let me go and grabbed my face, "Family is more important to me than slanging drugs. Look, I understand where your anger is coming fr—

"No! You don't! You didn't hurt like I did! The way you treated me," I shook my head, "Was unbelievable! You fucked me and sent me on my way, Vice. What kind of mess is that?

He pulled me into his chest and said, "I was hurting too, lil' mama. It killed me to have to treat you like that." he held my face in his hands again, "A diamond should never be mistreated the way I did you. You mean so fucking much to me, brown skin! Fuck! A nigga was just trying to protect you." He kissed me on the lips, "Understand that, shorty. Please. That shit I was spitting at you the other night... that wasn't real! I was trying to get you stop giving a fuck about me. Aight."

I exhaled. In the back of my mind I knew he didn't mean what he was saying. I was still very upset. I hated the fact that I was pregnant, though. A baby is the last thing either of us need. But by the look in his eyes, he was happy. He hated the circumstances but apparently he was willing to make the necessary changes for us to be a family.

I started to be a brat and ask him why he couldn't make the sacrifices he was talking about taking now, before finding out I was pregnant. But I changed my mind. Vice is in love with the game. His greed and overall hunger for money wouldn't allow him to pull out for anything other than a family. So, I shut my mouth and allowed him to love all over me. I swear, there was nothing like being in his arms. I felt complete. And, although this pregnancy was unwanted, by me of course, I was still excited about what the future may hold.

"First thing, you moving up out of that condo, shorty," said Vice as he stared at the positive results on the pregnancy test. "Hold up though, you pissed on this lil' mama?"

I giggled and said, "Of course, what the he—

He tossed it on the floor so fast, I went into a fit of laughter. Shit like this, I missed the most. I missed the dick too, but that couldn't compare to the overall feeling he gave me.

"Like I said though, I'm going to call a moving service to get your shit up out of there, aight?"

I nodded as I snuggled close to his chest, "I missed you, Vice."

He kissed me on my forehead and pulled me closer, "I missed you too, brown skin. Missing you had a nigga out here reckless. Murking shit off like the crazy nigga I am."

I looked up at him and said, "You're not a crazy nigga, Vice. I wish you could see you through my eyes."

He looked down at me and simply kissed me on the lips. I didn't think he was crazy, but what I thought didn't matter. Vice felt like he was a loose cannon, a crazy nigga with no limits. Sometimes he could be that but that's not what I saw when I looked at him. In the beginning, yeah, but almost a year in I felt the total opposite. When I looked at him, I saw a man who loved me with all of him. A man who treated me like a diamond. Someone who fought for what he wanted. He was just a stand up, real ass dude.

"Aight lil' mama. Let a nigga up. You getting fat already, damn," he joked as he pretended to struggle to lift me off of his chest.

I playfully slapped him and said, "Don't play." I got off of him and ran my fingers through my bundles, "What you about to do?"

"Make a couple moves, check on Lay," he told me as he stretched. And then he gave me a silly smile, "You carrying a nigga's seed and shit." He squatted down in front of me and rubbed my stomach, "Vice Jr. kicking back in that mothafucka huh?"

I laughed, "Um...our DAUGHTER will not be named Vice, thank you!"

His eyebrows wrinkled, "Fuck is you saying? I tore the pussy up! That's a savage growing in you. A king, my baby."

We joked around for a few more minutes before hopping in the shower together. Vice was really excited. I was worried. My parents were about to be grandparents of a child I conceived with a man they didn't like. The shit was sickening. I knew my mom would be okay. I was just worried about what Mack would say.

*

Two hours later, I was at the condo, sitting in the middle of my bedroom floor sorting clothes out. I couldn't believe the amount of clothes I had to donate. I came across so much old shit, I couldn't help but shake my head. My phone rung and I reached up on the bed and grabbed it. It was Jai.

I smiled and slid the green phone over, "Hey bab—

"Where you at? If you at the crib, leave and meet me at the mall. Right now," she said frantically.

I frowned up, "What is wrong with you?"

"Ugh, bitch did you just hear what I said?" I heard rubber burning in the background, "Fuck it, here I come. I'll be there in five minutes."

She hung up and I just stared at the phone. What the fuck is wrong with her? I called her back and she didn't pick up. I stood up and headed to the living room to unlock the door. Then I went into the kitchen for some orange juice. As soon as it hit my stomach, I got nauseos. I swear, I couldn't hold shit down. I ran to the bathroom and threw up into the toilet bowl.

"Storm!" I heard Jai yelling.

"I'm…" Gag. Urrrl. "In the bathroom." I told her in between throwing up.

She ran into the bathroom and covered her nose, "Bitch, you sick?"

"Pre…" Gag. Urrl. "Pregnant."

She stumbled back and leaned against the bathroom door, "Oh…oh my God. No. St—sis… call…call Vice right now! Now!" she yelled as she tried to pull me away from the toilet.

I fought her off as throw up hit the tiles on the bathroom floor, "Jai! Move! What.." Urrrrrl. "What is wrong with you!?"

I stood up, wiped my mouth with a tissue, and flushed the toilet.

She paced the bathroom floor, back and forth as I grabbed a Clorox wipe and cleaned my mess up.

"I fucked up. Shit! I fucked u! Call him sis! Please!"

I washed my hands, eyeing her in the mirror, "Bitch what did you do?"

"I had to," Jai cried. "It was either Vice or me."

I turned around so fast, and immediately wrapped my hands around her neck as I kept asking her what was going on. I was pissed. Jai was afraid. I didn't give a fuck. If she was on some snake shit, I wasn't going to hesitate ending her life right here in this bathroom. I love her, but I love myself first. If anything, she didn't love and care about me as much as she claimed. Before she got here she was rapping about how I needed to leave. Maybe she was more of a snake than I thought.

"Hold up! You told them about me bitch?" I asked her, cutting her off midsentence as she explained what she got herself into.

"I...I had to! That's why I'm trying to get you out of here. I didn't have a choice sis. He threatened to kill me—

"You could've came to us Jai! You know that shit!" I let her neck go and threw her against the door before storming out of the bathroom. I had to call my man and I prayed like fuck he answered. Vice stopped answering for me when he was out. He said I threw him off his game and it made him feel weak. I prayed he'd answer this one time. I needed him to.

12.

VICE

I ignored her call for the second time. Whatever brown skin wanted would have to wait. I was riding with Reek, on a mission to check up on a few houses. Apparently, niggas wasn't kicking out dough like they were supposed to. I was heated. If it was important, she'd shoot me a text. I tossed the phone in the middle compartment of my car, and shut it.

"What's the word on Luke," I asked Reek as I passed him the blunt.

"Weak nigga still posted in the city."

"Find out where he's resting. I have to tie up all loose ends."

He asked me why and I just turned the stereo up. He didn't need to know why. Like I said before, I didn't trust a mothafucking soul. Maybe I'll tell him why eventually, but the shit wasn't happening right now. I had too much to lose. I was wasting too much time on handling the Tech situation as is. I needed Reek to hit me off with that info before the day was out. Fuck cooking up a scheme. I was offing the pussy off rip.

177

Speaking of pussy, Olivia wouldn't stop calling me and I just hit that the night before. Bitch was already dickmatized. Thing is though, that shit is deaded. Now that I have my brown skin baby back in my life on some permanent official shit. Her pussy is the only pussy I'm blessing with this dick. Olivia's not a messy broad, but I won't give any woman the opportunity to speak ill about fucking with me while I'm seeing Storm. Side bitches aren't necessary when wifey's official.

Whatever these young niggas were over ere fucking up at to be dealt with. Considering the news I just got, I couldn't take any losses. Despite Storm being pregnant, though, taking a loss was never an option. Niggas knew I never took shortages, it's the principles.

Reek turned the stereo down to answer his phone. He told me it was his OG, hitting him up with Luke's location. She happily obliged. Mom dukes wanted them to patch up whatever beef that had going on that caused them to fall out. That was the furthest thing from my mind. Luke was about to get very acquainted with the bullets in my nine, though. That was for sure.

Beep. Beep. Beep!

I looked in my rearview mirror at the weak ass old head with dreads, flagging me down. I passed the blunt to Reek and slowed down a bit.

"Who is that, brodie?" Reek asked as he looked over his shoulder, out the back window.

I smirked as I pulled over, "Nigga, that's Mack!"

"Fuck his ho ass want?"

I sat my burner on my lap, "I don't know. But let's pray he's trying to pull some fuck shit. You already know how bad I want to add his body to the burner, my G."

Things should've changed when Storm told me she was carrying my child, right? Thing did change though. Now I wouldn't hesitate to send this old ass fuck nigga to his maker. If he's not willing and ready to finally accept the fact that I'm busting nuts all up in his daughter, then it's a must that I get rid of this nigga. I couldn't take the risk. I was tying up all loose ends. So, if his puss ass ain't trying to get with the program I'll make shit easier for him. I'm talking about taking him out of his misery. I'll happily raise my banger and penetrate his mental with the bullets in my clip. Storm would just have to get over it.

I shifted the car in park and waited on the nigga to come at my window. I was itching to murk his ass off the principles of what happened before. I chewed on my bottom lip, watching him walk up to my car through the rearview. I took the safety off the burner and hopped out before he could even get to my window.

"Ay, bro, what the fuck," yelled Reek just as I slammed the door shut.

I mobbed up to Mack with the burner on my side. He didn't seem intimidated at all. This nigga was irritating as hell! Swore up and down he was a fucking gangsta. Let me learn this nigga something real fast.

"No need for the banger, my nigga," he told me with his hands stuffed in the pockets of his Pelle.

I didn't stop walking until I was literally standing on his toes. Mack took a step back and chuckled like something was funny. I didn't give a fuck about the people in traffic watching. I couldn't give a tiny fuck about how many people could identify me in the police line up if I decided to cover the streets with his brains.

"Fuck you want, pussy," I asked him as I twisted my lips up. Mack kept laughing. I looked around and stepped closer to him, then pressed the barrel of the burner against his stomach. "What's funny?"

He stepped back and looked at me with fire in his eyes. His nose flared and my mission was accomplished. I wanted to piss the old nigga off. Wanted to put a lil' bit of fear in him. He was too fucking chill for me, like the shit I was on didn't bother him. It did.

"I'm only doing this shit for the sake of my daughter, homie! Thank God I ain't touched you boy!" yelled Mack as he turned off and headed for his Benz. He looked over his shoulder, "Let's talk!"

I chuckled and stuffed the burner in my waistband. I looked over my shoulder and Reek was standing outside of the whip with his hands up. I nodded at him and he got back inside. I chewed on the inside of my jaws as I treaded towards Mack whip.

I hopped inside before placing my gun back on my lap. No way in fuck was I about to sit beside a nigga who sent bullets flying my way not too long ago.

I stared at him as he turned the heat up and rubbed his hands together. He was cold, but the bullets in my gun would warm his ass right up. I kept reverting back to the thought of killing him. Right here. Right now. I wanted to leave the bitch nigga slumped over on the steering wheel.

Mack looked over at the gun on my lap and shook his head, and then blew into his hands. "That's your problem, right there." He said nodding at my pistol.

"Nah, this is the problem solver. Fuck you saying?"

He laughed, "You need stability. Limits."

I nodded, "I have limits, my G." I laughed, "Otherwise we wouldn't even be having this conversation right now. Unless you'd be able to speak from the grave."

Mack shook his head again, "I hate your young and reckless ass. Nothing but hate and animosity in my heart for you. But shit, my daughter love you so I have to respect that in order to get back in her good graces."

I know I said I would squash shit if he was willing to respect the fact that Storm and I were in love but I lied. I couldn't sit across from this fuck boy at Thanksgiving dinner. I couldn't imagine playing golf, shooting hoop, or any of that other weak nigga shit with him. Being fake just wasn't in my blood.

"Respect don't have to go both ways though. You sent bullets my way! I can't respect or let you breathe for much longer," I nonchalantly replied, never breaking eye contact with him.

"You threatening me?" asked Mack through his teeth.

"Promising you."

I looked around the outside of the car, peeping the scenery. Not too far from where we were sitting was a squad car with someone pulled over. I cursed myself for not having a silencer on this bitch. I bit down on my lip and turned my attention back to Mack.

He peeped the squad car and slickly pulled a pocket knife from his pocket. I jumped back as he swung it towards me.

"Gun's ain't the only way to kill, stupid young nigga," he told me as he kept swinging at me. I kicked him in the abdomen and he fell back against the door. I picked my burner up and smacked him across the face with it five times before he was knocked out cold. I glanced back at the squad car again, debating on if I should use his own knife on him. I decided against it. I know where the pussy nigga living. I'll be paying him a visit real soon.

I hopped out of the car and ran back to mine. I hopped in, snatched the car in drive and sped off.

"Fuck happened? You got blood all over yo self, bro!" yelled Reek.

I hadn't even noticed. I looked down at my shirt and back up at the road.

"Beat that nigga to sleep, that's what happened. Pussy pulled a knife out on me."

Reek sighed, "I was praying like fuck you didn't let off. I peeped them boys not too far from us."

I glanced at him, "I'm always aware my nigga. I peeped them too."

Fifteen minutes later, I pulled up at the spot. I was on seven mile, except this was a different house other than the one that stayed booming on Riopelle. This house didn't accumulate much money to begin with so for me to accept some type of shortage was a no go. I didn't give a fuck about the young cat working out of here promising me the rest in two days. Today is pay day, what the fuck do I care about two days from here? I don't.

Both me and Reek hopped out the whip and mobbed up the stairs and into the house. As soon as niggas laid eyes on me, their conversations came to a halt. Of course they were rapping about the young God. They peeped me coming way before I got here, about three blocks ago. Like I said, I kept cameras posted throughout the hood just in case five decided to fall through.

I sat on the beaten up black microfiber couch and kicked my feet up on the dirty coffee table.

"Let cha boy get a piece of gum, Petey. I know you got some." I said to him with a smirk. The stink breath nigga stayed with a pack of Big Red.

He went into the pocket of his Nike hoody and handed me a stick, "What's up, my nigga?" He said.

The other cats in the house followed suit.

I grabbed the gum and popped it into my mouth after pulling the wrapper off.

"You got that," I asked Petey as I chewed on the gum, staring him directly into his eyes. "And I mean, all of it. No shortages, my G."

He dramatically nodded his head, "Oh yeah, boss. I meant to hit your line and tell you everything was straight." He walked off and Reek followed behind him.

I kicked back on the couch, watching the big booty ho's twerking on the 20in flat screen. The other cats in the room sat there trying to play it off like they weren't watching a nigga. I was known to be impulsive. They were expecting me to lash out any minute now. Man all I was doing was trying to chill.

Out of clear blue, brown skin invaded my thoughts. I went into my pocket to retrieve my phone just to check up on her but I forgot I left it in the car. That was best. I'd hit her line as soon as we got up out of here. I didn't need to be seen speaking to my lady in front of these niggas anyway.

A few seconds later, Reek and Petey came from the back room carrying a duffle bag a piece. I stood up to leave and Petey extended his free hand to me. I looked

185

down at it, took the gum out of my mouth, and pressed it into the palm of his hand.

"Reek could've made this pick up without me. My time is precious, my mans. Today you wasted it."

Reek was cracking up laughing as we jogged down the steps, heading back to the whip.

"You's a mothafucking savage, bro." Reek said as we got inside of the car. "How the fuck you gone disrespect that man by putting your trif' ass chewed up on gum in his hand?" He was laughing so hard he could barely speak.

I laughed and glanced at him while pulling off, "Fuck 'em. He disrespected me by wasting me by wasting my time, dog."

I grabbed my phone from the middle compartment and called wifey back without even acknowledging the many text messages and calls from various people.

She picked up almost immediately after the phone started to ring.

"Wassup lil bab—

"Where are you? I've been calling like cr—

"I'm wrapping shit up right now." My low fuel light popped on. How the fuck? I just filled up the other day. I made a quick right into the nearby Sunoco gas station, "What's wrong, lil' mama?"

US AGAINST EVERYBODY: A DETROIT LOVE
TALE 3   MISS CANDICE

"Some niggas out to get y—

I interrupted her, "say no more. I'm on my shit, believe me. Head home and lock up."

"You're not hearing me, babe!" she cried, "I mean, right now. At this moment. Come...come home, please."

My eyes darted to the rearview. She had a nigga 'noid, thinking shit was about to pop off at this instance. But nothing was out of the ordinary.

"Calm down baby, aight? Stop crying." I handed Reek a bill and told him to grab some 'rillos and put fifty in the tank. He told me he was grabbing some shit too before hopping out. "But ay, where you get this information from?"

She was quiet. So quiet, that I had to repeat my question.

"Jai...they...I mean he...he made her do it."

She was hysterical. Cursing, who I figured was Jai out in the background. About how it's her fault and she couldn't believe she did this to her. That rat bitch? After I looked out for her on some one hundred shit with the Genie situation? She set a nigga up though? How the fuck is that for a thank you?

187

"Be cool, brown skin. I'll be there in a lil' bit, aight?"

"Okay. Please, be careful. I can't believe the audacity of this shady bitch." she paused, "But…you're not going to hurt her right?"

"Storm, stop talking. Chill out. I'll be there in a few. Stop bugging out."

I told her to go to the crib again before hanging up. I looked up and Reek was leaving out of the gas station with a bad redbone bitch in tow. Here this thirsty nigga go. He put the gas pump in the tank and walked over to my side of the car. He tapped on my window; I turned the key and let it down.

"What, pussy?" I jokingly asked him.

"Home girl needs a ride to the crib. I told her it was straight since we heading in that direction. Some bum niggas jacked her shit." Said Reek as he chewed on his honeybun.

"Fuck I look like, my mans?" I laughed and looked past him at the girl who was standing a few feet away, crying. "Captain save a thot? Fuck out of here, brodie."

I was on some play-play shit like wifey didn't just tell me some niggas were out to get me. I simply didn't give a damn. At the rate I was going, Mack will be added to the long list of niggas who wanted my head on a platter. What am I saying? Old head been wanting me dead since I winked at his 'princess'. When was there a time where a nigga wasn't out to get me? I can't live life worried about getting got. All I can do is stay on my P's and Q's and make sure I pull the trigger first.

"Come on bro. Look out for your man's on the one time." Reek leaned into my window and said, "I'm trying to get my dick wet. Feeeel me?"

I laughed and asked him where she stayed. He told me over on Watham near seven mile and Gratiot, by Robert's coney island. I nodded and said, "Aight, grab the thottie and escort her cry baby ass right to the back seat. Her stranger ass ain't riding shotgun with me."

He wiggled his eyebrows and said, "Hell nah she not. Best believe I'm kicking back in the backseat too."

"Thirsty nigga. Pass me the 'rillo."

I don't usually blow cigarillos but it was time for me to hit the weed stash and re-up on my personal supply.

He tossed the plastic grocery bag through the window and grabbed ol' girl's hand. He led her to my window and she thanked me. I just looked up at her and nodded before proceeding to rolling my bud up. Reek pulled the gas pump out of the tank once it was finished filling up and hopped right in the backseat. I shook my head, chuckled and sped off.

"So what happened, my baby," Reek asked the girl who was busy looking down at her phone.

She looked up, glanced at me looking at her in the rearview, and then over to Reek. "I was just minding my business when a group of three young guys pulled a gun out on me and told me to give them my stuff. I had been standing around that gas station for twenty minutes and no one would help."

I made a right turn and started to laugh, "That's what happened huh?"

Reek leaned over the seat and said, "What's popping bro? You on that 'noid shit as usual?"

The girl leaned back on the seat. I stopped at a red light, turned around, and stared into her face. She wouldn't make eye contact with me, and was fidgety as hell. She kept that phone in her hand, texting. Shorty looked familiar as hell. I never forgot a face. I was having a hard time putting her face on a place though. I couldn't recollect where I knew her from but I knew her.

As I sat there, unblinkingly staring at her, something else was brought to my attention.

"Br—

I interrupted Reek by grabbing the girl by her face and making her look at me, "You've gotta be the stupidest bitch living." I snatched the phone from her, "How is it that you say you got robbed but...but they ain't take the iPhone 6 plus up off of you?"

I grabbed her neck and threw her back against the leather seat.

"Erotic," I said to her with a smirk on my face before turning around to pull away from the green light.

Reek snapped, "Dirty bitch, brodie?!" I nodded and he backhanded her, "Fuck is you doing out here? Don't you know you messing around with some real, stone-cold, don't give a fuck niggas you bum bitch."

Shorty was far from a bum bitch though. Whoever sent her my way should've known better than to send one of the most paid stripping bitches at Erotic City my way on some set up shit. And to let the bitch keep her phone after telling me she was robbed? Stupid. Amateur. It's cool though. I'm still taking this bitch to the crib, even though I know that's not where she stay, simply because I know that's where she was told to lure me to. Today had already been fun, but a little more fun won't hurt nothing.

I wasn't even as mad as I should've been. You know I don't give a fuck. So I grabbed my phone and switched to Doughboyz Cashout Set up Bitch. Turned the volume to the max and stared at her through the rearview.

Can't lie, baby girl is a sexy bitch
Can't trust her, she a set up bitch
So many niggas in the hood tried to bless the bitch
But fell short, she a set up bitch

Now Shut up bitch, get off the phone and stop texting
And quit playing around girl and get the undressing
She hit the bathroom, that ass look impressive
Bout to beat it up, beat it up in my necklace
I knocked on the door, she like hol up nigga wait?
What's taking so long, I ain't got time to play
Tryna hit and quit it, I ain't got time to stay
Came out fully clothed, I'm like where the lingerie
So like red lobster, bitch got to acting fishy
Lookin out the window, realizing it hit me
She a set up bitch, a set up bitch
But I ain't slipping tho, you know I got Barrettas and
shit...

A couple of minutes later I pulled into up in front of the raggedy ass house she told me she stayed at. I sat in the middle of the street so niggas could get a good look at me. I turned around and went through her phone to see who she was texting. The name TECH stood out big as day. Tech... in other words Luke. Bitch was rapping to him about how it was easy to get a nigga and shit. I turned the music down and laughed. Told Reek his cousin was behind the shit, and posted up in the building right fucking now. He went for the door handle but I stopped him.

"Hold up bro, let's tie up some loose ends real quick," I let the windows down because I knew he was watching.

And then I called him. When he picked up, I turned the volume back up. I smiled, turned around, aimed my banger at her head, and let off a shot. Reek jumped out of surprise, and pushed the girl's lifeless body off of him. Bro had brains and shit all over him.

13.

JAI

When I saw Bunz head fall over, handing out of the window with a big ass hole where her facial features once were, I stumbled back away from the window and into Tech. He roughly pushed me away and I fell onto the floor. I sat there on my knees, sobbing uncontrollably. This nigga Vice is about to end my life so fucking scandalous. I know what kind of treatment snake bitches get. I don't even know why I thought Vice would even fall for that weak ass scheme.

"Get up and grab one of those choppers, bitch." Tech yelled as he gave me a swift kick to the ribs.

I grabbed onto my side and let out a cry. He told me to get up again, so I did as I was told so I wouldn't get another kick. I walked over to the window and hurled when Reek kicked Bunz lifeless body out into the streets. My eyes darted from one end of the block to the other. I cursed under my breath. There wasn't a soul out on the block. It was freezing out. Had it been the summertime, Vice wouldn't have even been on this reckless shit.

Reek hopped back in and before he could close the door completely, Vice was backing up to position the car to drive up into the driveway. He stopped and shifted the car in drive when he was perfectly aligned with the driveway. What happened next was unbelievable. He came towards the house at full speed. Once I realized he had no plans of stopping, I backed away from the window.

We were at a small, raggedy wood and vinyl ranch house with no stairs, so I wasn't surprised a few seconds later when Vice's challenger came crashing into the got damn living room. Tech was too busy loading guns to react and was hit. He should've been prepared a long time ago, fucking with a crazy nigga like Vice. The goons he had with him were gunned up, ready for war. Vice and Reek were outnumbered. 5 against 2. 6 if you counted me. But trust, a bitch ain't stupid enough to participate in a gun war against these two nutty niggas. Fuck what Tech was rapping about. Plus, these niggas are like family to me. The only reason I did what I did was because Tech threatened to kill me.

"Grab that fucking chopper, stupid bitch." Yelled Tech as he slowly recovered, coming my way.

I fanned smoke and debris out of my face as I went running to the back of the house. I looked over my shoulder and Vice and Reek were stepping out of the busted ass car.

And then, the gun fire erupted. I could literally hear bullets whizzing past my ears. I was terrified. I had never been in this type of situation. This was some straight up

195

gangsta, thug shit. Things weren't even supposed to go like this. Bunz was supposed to text Tech when they pulled up. She was supposed to get out of the car and when she did, they were going to light Vice's car up with bullets. But that didn't happened. When, who we thought was Bunz but ended up being Vice, called we were all caught off guard. The terror that washed over Tech's face when he answered the phone told me then that I was on the wrong side of shit.

I should've known that shit from the get go. Now I'm stranded at this mothafucka, in some serious danger. Tech ended up picking me up. After Storm went off on me, I cried myself home. And then, to make matters worse, when I pulled up at the crib Tech was sitting in his car waiting on me. He's a sick bastard and wanted me to watch him ki—

"Where you think you going, bitch?" I looked over my shoulder and stopped dead in my tracks after witnessing the size of the gun one of Tech's goons had pointed in my face.

I held my hands up and closed my eyes tightly as tears rolled down my cheeks. Why couldn't I be with Ryan right now? A bitch was finally changing for the better and look at what's happening. Maybe this is Karma for all of the fucked up shit I did in the past. Whatever the case, I didn't think I deserved to die this way. I was only trying to survive!

"Bitch, you coming wi—

US AGAINST EVERYBODY: A DETROIT LOVE
TALE 3   MISS CANDICE

The way his blood and brains painted the walls and my face sent me into shock. I saw the bullet exit the side of his head and everything. I stood there screaming at the top of my lungs until Reek cracked me over the head with the same gun he just murdered ol' boy with.

*

The speeding of the car I woke up in jerked me awake.

"Ho, you keep calling me for dick but you ain't trying to look out for a nigga. I told you, look out and I'll pipe you on the regular, aight?" yelled Vice into his phone.

This mothafucka cheating on my sister? Despite the fucked up position I was in, I tried to lash out and smack him in the back of his head. But, they had my wrists zip tied. I threw my head back against the seat and almost threw up. Right beside me was brain matter that once belonged to Bunz.

I closed my eyes and silently cried. I didn't know what was about to happen to me. Reek looked over his shoulder at me lying down on the seat, crying my eyes out and said, "Ho, shut your snake in the grass ass up."

"Don't talk to me like you're out of your mothafuckin mind, nigga! I'm not a snake bitch! That nigga threatened to take my fucking life if—

"Jai, shut the fuck up before I shut you up. You're the only bitch I know who still talk tough knowing you're about to be a goner out to this bitch." Yelled Vice after ending his phone conversation.

I started to say some slick shit about the bitch he was just on the phone with talking about sticking dick to but I decided against it. A reminder of what he'd do to me was sitting literally a couple inches away from me. Instead, I decided to beg and plead for my life. Vice must have some type of soft spot for me in his heart right? He didn't leave me back there leaking with them other niggas.

"Please, Vice, understand where I was coming from," I cried, "You would've done the same thing."

"Nah, my baby, see I'm the definition of a real nigga. The last of a dying fucking breed. I would've told that weak ass nigga to suck a dick, and plugged my nigga with the info so he could body 'em off top. Ratting and turning yo back on a mothafucka who's looked out for you is some soft ass sucka, bitch shit." He yelled as he sped down the road. "Dig me?!"

"Vice! I'm not cut out for this shit! You gotta have some kind of love for me right? You ain't gon ki—

"Put a pause on that shit." He said before laughing, "Don't even mistake this little joy ride for me being compassionate or any of that other soft shit. If it was up to me, I would've shot ya fuckin face off back at that trap them other cats died up in. Wifey shot me a text...told me she wanted to at least see you again before I snatched the life up out you." He paused, "So you see... this is for her. Not you, you bottom of the barrel ass bitch."

I nodded as reality slowly crept in. There was nothing I could do. Storm could've but apparently she didn't give a damn about me anymore. That pained me the most. Storm seemed to be cool with Vice killing me. She didn't care. I mean... in a way I understood but hell, why couldn't anyone understand that I had to do what I did?

14.

STORM

One again, my life was a complete fucking mess.

On my way to Vice's –well our – house, Mack called my phone hysterically yelling about how he's going to 'holla at Vice'. At this point, I'm over all of the bullshit. He kept going on and on about how he tried to reconcile whatever beef they had going on for the sake of restoring our relationship. But Vice was on another tip, the murder tip to be precise. I simply told him to leave it alone. I told him to give me some time. He thought Vice was the reason our relationship wassn't the same. But he's the one to blame for that.

After hanging up with him, I noticed an unmarked police car trailing me. They stayed behind me until I took the exit for home. From the looks of things, it was definitely a female. Off top, I knew it was the bitch who had it out for Vice. Like he said before, he's probably going to have to get rid of her.

So, now, I'm at the crib impatiently biting on my gel nails, pacing the floor. Of course, Vice wasn't answering his phone. He did text to tell me he was straight and how he had 'ol girl' with him. Ol girl being Jai. I asked him to bring her here first but he didn't reply. In the back of my mind, I knew he killed her especially since he wasn't picking up. Vice wasn't going to let her live. After what she's done, she deserves whatever it is she has coming her way. As much as it hurts admitting that, Jai knew she was going against a savage ass nigga. She knew death was an option when she decided to go against the grain.

I shouldn't have even disrespected him like that by asking him to spare her life. I was using the fact that Vice had a soft spot in his heart for me, to my advantage. If I don't allow him to get his revenge he'll forever blame me for whatever feelings he'll harbor behind not doing it.

My phone rang, *Carla.*

I have missed yet another day of work. Too much was going on. My mind was on too much bullshit to even have room to think about work.

"Hey," I dryly answered.

"What's going on, boo? I'm giving you the benefit of the doubt because of everything you've been going through but you haven't even called me."

"I know, Carla, and I appreciate you for that. Things have been more crazier than ever." I shook my head because as badly as I didn't want to quit, I knew I had to. "I have to sort some things out in my life, boo. Work doesn't fit into my life right now. I just found out I'm preg—

"Ohhh wait a got damn minute, bitch. Fuck Nordstorm. How could you not tell me that before?"

I sighed and looked out of the window as I noticed Vice pulling up in Reek's car. Where in the hell is the Challenger?

"We'll talk later, okay?" I told Carla hating that I've been blowing her off so much lately.

"Okay, hun. Please call. I miss you. Hell, I even miss Jai," she laughed.

I cringed and then we said our goodbyes. I rushed to the front door just as they were getting out of the car. I opened the door and stood there with my arms crossed over my chest. When I got a good look at Vice, my stomach dropped. I gasped ad took off running down the stairs towards him.

His shirt was heavily stained with blood. So much blood that you wouldn't be able to tell he was wearing a white tee.

"Wha...where...where are you hit, Vice," I screamed frantically, looking all over his body.

He had the nerve to smile at me, "Wassup brown skin baby? You look good as fuck, girl."

TALE 3   MISS CANDICE

I looked over at Reek and he just shook his head. Jai...I ignored that crying bitch. I grabbed Vice by his arm to help him into the house.

"Where are you hit, Vice?" I yelled.

"I got this, baby. Don't even trip." He told me as he pulled the tee over his head. "Plus, most of this blood ain't even mine." He winked with a sly smile.

I covered my mouth at the sight of the huge hole in his upper arm, gushing with blood.

"Reek, come to the back with me my nigga," Vice said.

"No! I'll help you." I shouted as I started to follow behind him.

"Nah, lil mama, I need to discuss something with bro. Say your good-byes to that shiesty bitch." he looked me square in the eyes as he said, "Because it will be the final good-bye, Storm."

I just nodded. He was shot. He could've been killed. And it was all Jai's fault.

"So, you gone let your cheating ass nigga threaten to kill your sister, Storm?" Jai yelled.

I totally ignored the fact that she mentioned the word cheater and nigga in the same sentence, referring to my Vice. She was trying to throw me off. She was trying to place the heat on someone other than her, if only for a second. Jai could say Vice was fucking a million bitches behind my back and in this moment, I wouldn't give a fuck.

"Jai, shut the fuck up." I screamed. "Ever since we met, I've been dealing with your shit. Saving you! Having your back and all. But the one time you were supposed to take care and save me. When it mattered the most... you not only ratted on my man, you told them how to find me too!" I screamed as tears fell from my eyes.

Vice, who was once on his way to the bathroom, stopped dead in his tracks. Fear washed over Jai's face as he turned around and charged at her like a raging bull. Jai took off running to the front door. When she opened it, two women in skull caps barged in holding guns that looked like some shit straight out of the movie, Scarface.

They knocked her to the floor, stumbling over her body as they tried to come after us. Which gave us a chance to run away, to the back of the house. Me, Reek, and Vice stayed behind the bedroom door. Vice quickly rushed to the closet where the guns were. He tossed Reek a big gun. He snatched a designer shirt off of a hanger and tightly wrapped it around his gunshot wound. I stood there, heavily panting, in shock as the running got closer and closer.

"Storm, get away from the door," whispered Reek as Vice loaded his guns.

He looked over to me, ran over, and hurriedly pulled me into the baster bathroom inside of the room.

I snapped out of it and whispered, "Give me a gun. I can...I can help."

Vice looked at me like I lost my mind, "You gon' lie your beautiful ass in that bathtub, aight? And wait on me to come back for you."

"But what if you do—

He placed his finger over my lips and said, "I'm coming back. I promise." He kissed my lips and told me he loved me before I could say another word.

BOOM! TAT. TAT. BLAH. BLAH. BLAH.

It seemed like the shots rang off as soon as he closed the bathroom door. I hurried to the tub, climbed inside, and covered my eyes to muffle the echoic sounds of gunfire. I closed my eyes tightly and cried, praying God spared Vice's life.

I couldn't believe Jai had done this to me...to us! Those bitches outside of the door were out to get me! They must've followed me from my house. What if I had been alone? I wouldn't have known how to find the guns. I would've been naked and vulnerable. I would've been DEAD! Jai didn't give a fuck about me so why should I give a fuck about her?

And then, the house fell silent. I pulled the shower curtain in an attempt to hide. A few seconds later, I heard the bathroom door creek open. I covered my mouth, to muffle my heavy breathing. But my heart was beating so hard and fast that I was sure whoever entered the bathroom heard it beating against my chest.

The curtain was snatched open. Immediately, I kicked and threw punches.

"Wait... hold up lil' mama!" yelled Vice as he pulled me into his arms. "Relax baby, it's me." He held my face in his hands and said, "I told you I was coming back. No way in fuck was I going to let them bitches come in here and...and hurt you." He touched my stomach, "Forever...til the death of me...I'll protect you and my child. I'll never let anyone hurt y'all aight?!"

I couldn't control my breathing as I nodded and buried my face into his bare chest as I cried.

"Where's...where's Jai?" I managed to ask as I looked up at him.

His hazel brown eyes glossed over with nothing but rage. The softness he stared at me before washed away at the mention of Jai.

He grabbed my hand, stood behind me, and covered my eyes. And then he led me out of the bathroom and into the living room. When he removed his hands from my eyes, I stared at Jai who was now zip-tied to a dining room chair. Vice stood before her with a pistol in his hand.

"This was you too? Asked Vice as he menacingly stared down at her.

Jai kept her wet eyes on me as tears rapidly spilled down her cheeks. I couldn't help but feel an overwhelming sadness in my heart. She licked her dry lips and told me she loved me. For as long as I could remember, Jai has been in my life. I ran over to her and kissed her on the cheek before telling her I loved her too. I hugged her body as tightly as I could while we both boohooed in each other's arms.

BLAH!

I stood back and watched as Jai's head fell over to the side with blood leaking from her temple.

I handed Vice his gun back before walking out of the house.

15.

REEK

It had been a month since all of that crazy shit popped off. A niggas soul was finally at peace after murking off my own cousin. Fuck him. It was either him or us. And of course I chose me. He didn't care about the blood we shared, so why should I? Dog, I was just sick and tired of giving the shit thought. So I pushed it to the back of my mind. Even as I stood at the closed casket funeral, consoling my moms, sister, and his sisters. Tyreeka kept staring at me the whole time. She was on some 'twin' shit. She felt bad vibes and knew off rip that I was the one that sent that bullet ripping through the flesh on his face. I never confessed it to her. I didn't have to.

Anyway, like I said, I pushed that shit in the back of my mind and focused on the happiness in front of me. Laila. Baby girl is official as fuck. We were sneaking around like kids, but I didn't give a fuck. I was just happy to be blessing my dick with some good ass, bomb ass pussy for a change. To be honest, it was more than just pussy. I couldn't understand why the dude she was with before beat on her. I couldn't imagine why a woman as good as she is would be treated so poorly. Like now, her sexy ass is sitting as breakfast tray in my lap. Breakfast in bed for a nigga!

I dug into the cheesy, sugary grits. I told her my favorite foods on our first date and she hadn't forgot a thing. She paid attention. Took notice. Took care of all of a niggas needs. Like now for instance. She's under the sheets right now, wetting my dick up with her thick ass warm saliva. A niggas really eating breakfast in bed, getting head. Man, this is the fucking life.

She peeked her head from up under the sheets and smiled, "How are the grits, Tyreek?"

I smiled and licked the spoon clean, "Best I ever had. Even better than mom's." I paused, "don't tell her I said that shit though, aight?"

After only a month, I had even introduced her to the family. Like I said, she's official. I haven't been this serious about a female since my ex Asia. Not a woman on earth can compare to Asia. I don't think there's anybody capable of having me as open as she had me.

I planned on telling Vice about us today. I was sick and tired of sneaking around like a little fucking boy, hiding a relationship from parents. I should've said something sooner though. Because now that their relationship had gotten better, I didn't know how he was going to take me smashing his sister. They were tight as hell now.

US AGAINST EVERYBODY: A DETROIT LOVE
TALE 3   MISS CANDICE

Bro told me about having Olivia do a check on her. Everything came back squeaky clean so that there told him he could open up to her. After finding out she was straight, he hung up the phone and let out a sigh of relief. He called Laila right after and went to the fucking movies. I was low key happy for them. They had gone so long without each other that it was apparent that they spent hella time together. Being in the same room with them was awkward as hell. For Laila too. Most of the time, I had to leave the room or some shit. I couldn't be in the same room with her without wanting to fuck all over her.

She giggled and came from up under the covers. She laid beside me, and rested her head on my shoulder.

"I'm happy I met you, Tyreek. You make me really happy," said Laila.

I looked over at her, expecting to see a smile on her face. Instead, she looked sad.

"If I make you happy, why you ain't smiling, girl?" I joked.

She shrugged and kissed me on the cheek before climbing out of bed, "No reason. I'm about to take a shower. Vice has some business to take care of, so I'm going to Storm's doctor's appointment with her."

I nodded and finished off my breakfast, confused.

Ten minutes later, I was flickering through the channels, when I heard talking coming from the bathroom. I looked in that direction, waved it off, and turned my attention back to the TV. After a while, the shit started to bug me. I sat the tray to the side, and pulled the white linen off of my body before quietly creeping out of the bed.

When I got to the bathroom she was on her way out, with a smile on her face, hands behind her back.

"Who were you talking to?" I asked with a frown on my face. In my line of work, everybody is suspicious. I don't give a fuck about how good the pussy is. Or who she shared a bloodline with. As you can see, none of that shit even mattered.

"Vice. What's wrong with you?"

I gave her the 'what the fuck ever' look with my head cocked back a little, "Shit. What was that nigga talking about?"

She draped her arms over my shoulder and ran her fingers through my dreads with her freehand, "You need your hair twisted up. You know…I can do them for you."

US AGAINST EVERYBODY: A DETROIT LOVE
TALE 3   MISS CANDICE

When Laila spoke to me, she stared me in the eyes. A nigga can't even lie; her light brown eyes had me captivating. Not only that, her beauty is regal. She had an exotic look to her. Curly hair, light skin, dimples...man shorty is just cold as hell. The baddest I've ever fucked with.

"Aight, twist me up when you finish up with Storm, baby," I told her as I licked my lips, pretending to be falling for her bullshit. Yeah, Laila's got game but she ain't fooling me. How is she talking to Vice and that nigga on a mission nobody but me knows about? Plus, she just told me herself that he was busy. When bro is busy, he don't pick up. I had a feeling this stupid broad was back fucking with the nigga Vice caught going Ike on her at the gas station.

She kissed me on the lips, and turned around on her toes, to go back into the bathroom. I watched as she sat her phone on the counter before she got into the shower. I walked away from the door, but just enough to be out of eyesight in case she decided to get one last look at me before she closed the curtain.

When I heard the curtain being pulled, I quietly reentered the room. Hell yeah a nigga was about to go snooping. No way in fuck was this broad about to have me catching feelings just to go carry her ass back to the old dude. I picked the phone up an unlocked the screen. I walked out of the bathroom when I pulled her call log up and punched the number she just dialed, into my own phone. I went back into the bathroom to sit her phone back where it was before I hit the call button on my own shit.

"Detective Olivia Thompson speaking."

I hung up and stood there in shock for a lil' bit. After the shock though, the savage in me kicked in and I headed back to the bathroom. But I stopped in my tracks before storming in there on some animal shit. I had to play this smart. If there was a time to tell bro what the fuck was popping off between his sister and I, this was it. I couldn't just murk this bitch off the strength of finding out she knew Thompson. I had to have proof. As tight as she and Vice are now, that nigga would never believe me without it.

"Baby?"

I walked a few feet away from the door and yelled, "Wassup?"

"Can you bring my towel in?"

I was itching to kill this bitch. I bit down on my lips, thinking about choking the life out of her. My mouth literally salivated at the urge of killing this bitch, no lie. Not only was she out to get Vice, she was out to get me too. Bitch sat up sucking my dick, fucking me, feeding me, all that wifey shit just to hook a nigga. That's exactly what she did too. Mission accomplished, you shiesty ass bitch.

I grabbed her towel off of the bed and took it to the bathroom. I sat the toilet seat down and sat on top of it.

"Oh, you came to chill with me huh," she joked with her head peeking from behind the curtain.

I wanted to grab the lid from the back of the toilet and bash her fucking head in with it. Bitch just didn't know how heated I was.

I smiled at her and said, "I just want to chop it up with you before you head out. Ay, you said you just talked to bro?"

She closed the shower curtain, "Yeah but he hurried off the phone because Storm was throwing up." She laughed, "Morning sickness is kicking her ass."

"Shut the fuck up, lying, lil' bitch," I mumbled.

"Huh?"

"Nothing. What time is the appointment?"

"I think twelve. I'm going to call her."

Fuck out of here. Thinking back on it, Vice would never miss a doctor's appointment. No way in hell he'd be on a murder mission knowing Storm had an appointment. Laila's a fucking liar.

"Aight." I told her as I got up from the seat. I stood there, staring at the shower curtain. Damn. I really liked this bitch. I guess it's back to fucking with Keisha's thot ass until something real comes along. At least she's thorough and I don't have to worry about her being a snake.

*

Like I said, there was no way in hell bro would miss a doctor's appointment. I'm sitting behind the wheel of my 'lac watching Laila enter a small, diner wearing a skull cap, scarf, and sunglasses to conceal her identity. She kept looking over her shoulder on some paranoid shit. There were times when I thought she peeped me inconspicuously sitting a few businesses down from the diner.

Ten minutes later, Detective Olivia Thompson pulled up in front of the diner and got out. I shook my head as I watched the bitch walk in the restaurant and sit across from Laila who had the menu up to her face.

I pulled my phone from my coat pocket and called bro. He had to be finished with his mission by now since two hours had passed. After a couple of rings, he picked up.

"What it is, fam?"

"I got some shit to put in your ear. Meet a nigga on at the Royal Gril on E. Warren."

"Aight. I'm right around there way. Be there in about give, my nigga." We hung up and I sat there watching the door, hoping like hell bro came before they dipped.

Titanic on my wrist, bad bitch on my dick
Did a donut in the 6, I just drove by Magic City
Put the heron in the bricks, put the heron in the bricks
Put the heron in the bricks, ain't nothing change, I got it
On a worldwide treasure hunt, blowin' good Guinea
Pretty girls reppin' "Pretty Gang" fuckin' wit the kiddo
Type to fuck a hood nigga good, then tell em "ditto"
Went from 5 on the indo, 30 rounds in the extendo
Fuck a friend though, ain't pretend though
Nigga comin' through sprayin' at the window
Get the memo, got a line, on Chyna White
But I ain't giving out no info
Get to bendin' corners like a nigga ridin' in a limo
I been in the pussy all day, at the cribbo

I fuck a bitch, she tell her friend, I love some free promo
I love a freak ho tho...

I sat back as Future's Freak Hoe played at a low volume thinking. As I thought back on the time we spent together, certain things that didn't make sense before, made perfect sense now. She always talked about these job interviews she went to, but when I asked her how it went she'd look lost, not knowing what I was talk about. And then, after refreshing her memory – which I shouldn't have had to when the bitch seemed excited as fuck about getting called for the interview in the first place – she'd smack herself in the head like it skipped her mind. Not only that, though. She told me on countless occasions that she was going to some domestic violence meetings and shit during the week. But when we'd link up later on the day she claimed to attend a meeting, she never mentioned it. Shit, I know, that there should've told me something but I thought maybe she was a little slow from my mans beating the shit out of her.

Speaking of that nigga, even her stories about him didn't make sense. She went from being his bitch for three years, to just meeting him a couple of months ago. He went from beating her every day to, only doing it when she ticked him off. Like I said, I thought she was just missing a couple of screws. Her stories about her childhood was a little off too. I didn't really give a fuck about anything she was saying for real anyway. I was more focused on getting my dick wet. Talking to Laila did nothing but make me horny. The way her mouth moved, her perfect lips, and wet tongue… dog…a nigga was whipped. That's probably why I didn't give a fuck too much neither. But what happened today…I couldn't let that shit slide.

Five minutes later, like clockwork, Vice was parking behind me in his new Dodge Charger R/T. A couple seconds later he hopped in and slapped hands with me.

"What's the word?" he asked looking vexed. I knew the mission he was on earlier was eating at him. He's really about to flip once he finds out Laila is affiliated with Thompson. Everything Thompson told him lost it's crediabilty as soon as she answered that phone earlier.

"Keep your eyes on the door, my ni—

"Stop fucking around dog. What the fuck is up? You think I want to be sitting here playing the guessing game? I'm trying to get back home to wifey. Lil' mama sick as fuck. I'd—

I nodded to the restaurant and said, "Chill nigga. There's part of your questi—

"What do I give a fuck about Detective Olivia having lunch? What's suspect about a bitch being hungry?"

I laughed, "Man… shut the fuck up and peep game nigga! I'm not wasting yo time bro, on moms.

Vice shifted in his seat, stuffed his hands in the pocket of his coat, and stared at the restaurant frowning with wrinkled eyebrows. The nigga was just hot about the shit he just did a minute ago. Taking his frustrations out on me because I'm probably the first person he's talked to since the shit popped off. I told him before he went on that mission that it wasn't going to be as easy as he thought it was.

"There you fucking have it." I told him as I punched the steering wheel.

He sat up and narrowed his eyes, "That's Lay?" I nodded and he said, "Fuck is she doing talking to Olivia?"

"My thoughts exactly."

16.

STORM

I swallowed the fear in the form of a lump, in my throat and cut the car off. As I stared up at my ma's house the fear returned. How was I going to address the questions they were about to ask me. Jai's murder was one I was having a really hard time coming to grips with and I knew I'd be bombarded with questions about how I was holding up about it. Everyone thought Jai was just randomly killed by a serial killer who had already been picking off women in the city. I guess we lucked up with that one. Still, with no suspicion on me, I beat myself up about it more than I'd like to. She was my best friend. My sister. But she had to die. And I felt that it was my responsibility to pull the trigger. I wouldn't allow myself to sit back and just watch Vice take her away from me. I wanted to do it. It was easier for me that way.

I'm not here for that though. I'm here to tell my family I'm carrying the bastard child of a man they dislike. I'm sure my momma will be excited, but Mack? Tuh! That's a whole other story. He and Vice still have issues. I even thought about trying to get them to see eye-to-eye myself. But the both of them are stubborn and probably will never get along. Hell, I've still been stubborn too. I couldn't allow myself to fix the relationship with Mack. As you can see, he still haven't gained my trust enough to call him daddy. I'm over it. The only reason I'm even telling him is because he's the grandfather. I don't even know if I want him around my child. His hate is so strong for Vice that there's no telling what he'd do. I know that might sound crazy to you but did you forget he had The Crazy Horse shot up, knowing I was inside? I don't put anything past him. And my primary focus as a parent is to protect my baby.

I grabbed my designer bag off of the passenger seat and got out of the car. I put the bag over my shoulder and held my pea coat tightly close. The weather was frigid; it couldn't have been no more than 10 degrees out. The snow was deep and my mom hadn't shoveled her snow. Thank God I wasn't on any cutesy shit today and decided to rock my Nike boots. As I stood on the porch, stomping snow off my boots, my mom opened the door.

"Hey sweetie." She said, welcoming me with open arms.

I gave her a hug and she stepped aside to let me in. The aroma of fried chicken hit my nose and my stomach growled almost immediately. I wanted to run in the kitchen and grab me a few pieces but with the way my morning sickness is set up, I decided against it. I wasn't even supposed to be out today. I had plans of being catered to by my boo all day. But once he called saying he had some other things to tie up, I decided I'd get dressed and share the news with my parents.

"What you cooking," I asked her as I kicked my boots off at the door.

"That's your daddy. He's cooking wing dings and pasta salad," she told me with the side-eye. "Trying to win you back with food."

I love wing dings, and I absolutely love pasta salad.

"It's going to take a lot more than food to make up for the way he's been acting." I told her as we walked to the kitchen.

He had the nerve to be standing at the stove in my mom's apron, dumping wingdings into the deep fryer. He looked over his shoulder and nervously smiled at me. I returned the same look and said hi. After wiping his flour coated hands on the front of the apron, he walked over to me with open arms. I tensed up when he hugged me. I hadn't hugged him in I don't know how long. I was having a hard time forgetting about what he did. He was making an effort but I just wasn't ready to let go yet. The shootout happened about four months ago but it still bothers me a lot. He should be happy I'm even in the same room with him. In the beginning, I wouldn't even do that.

"You look pretty, princess." Said Mack before kissing me on the forehead and walking back to the stove.

I twisted my lips and sat at the kitchen table with my momma.

"He know I'm a grown woman right?" I whispered.

She giggled, "You'll always be his princess; even when you're fifty."

"He needs to learn to let go." I seriously told her, "That's what messed out relationship up to begin with."

"I can hear you, Storm." Said Mack turning towards us. "Understand that I'm trying, aight?"

I took my pea coat off and hung it on the back of my chair. I nodded and told him okay. My moms stood up and ran her fingers through my hair. I needed it done but since I've been so sick, I barely wanted to leave the house. Carla and I planned on hitting the shop together later.

"What's going on with this head of yours," she asked with a smirk on her face. "You look different."

I laughed and moved her hands out of my hair, "What are you talking about ma?"

She stood in front of me with her lips twisted up, "Mmhmm. I already know."

My stomach filled with butterflies just as Mack sat a plate of wingdings in front of me. I looked down at the plate, wanting to dig right into it. The both of them stood there watching me like crazy people. Mack was waiting to see what I thought of his chicken. My momma? I didn't know what her point was.

"What's wrong, princess?" asked Mack with worry wrinkles covering his forehead.

"Yeah, what's wrong *princess*?" asked my mom, adding extra emphasis on princess. She was being goofy but I didn't think anything was funny.

"Nothing. It looks good…"

"I know that much. I want to know how you think they taste. You haven't had my chicken in years." Said Mack smiling.

My momma stood there with her arms folded over her chest, "Sick?"

I rolled my eyes and looked away. "I'm pregnant."

I didn't want to tell them like that but I didn't have a choice. They were all in my face.

Mack simply walked away while my momma excitedly jumped up and down.

"I knew you were pregnant when you came and got your eyebrows threaded the other day," she yelled. "Mmmhm, momma knows honey!" She waved Mack off, "Don't stunt him. He'll get over it. How far along are you?"

She was a lot happier than I expected. I don't think she cared at all about who the father was. What mattered to her was that her daughter was giving her a grandchild and that spoke volumes to me. Mack is too damn childish and full of himself to even think like that.

"Just 10 weeks." I looked over to Mack and he was taking the apron off, on his way out of the kitchen. "And you wonder why I'd rather not speak to you."

He turned around and yelled, tight-lipped, "Storm! Don't." he pointed at me, "Don't talk to me right now, aight?" He walked out of the kitchen and I heard him mumble, "Can't be that fucking stupid."

"And you can't be stupid enough to even think I would want to reconcile our relationship. You're more of a monster than Vice will ever be." I snatched my coat from the back of my seat and stood up. "I'm having a child with a great man. He'll be a better father to our child than you were to me! He'd never do what you did to me, to our child!"

"Wait a minute, Storm. Let him leave. Stay with me. I'm not understanding why I have to go without seeing you because of his immaturity!" yelled my mom. "Mack, get the hell out."

"You gon' sit up and let this little girl speak to me this way," he yelled, coming our way. "That nigga is turning you against me!"

I didn't back away like I did before at the hospital when Jai was hurt. Nah, see I'm a different woman now. And Mack doesn't intimidate me at all.

"Who you think you is sticking your lil' chin and shit out at?" he frowned, "Storm I will—

"You will *what?*" I asked with nothing but venom spilling from my tongue. "Threaten me and I swear to God not only will you have a problem with me... you'll have an even bigger with my man!"

Okay, okay. I was tripping but I had to let his ass know! Again, he's my father but lately he's been acting like everything but that. But still, I was going too far and even my momma had to tell me to chill out. I apologized to her before storming out of the door. I let her know that I'll be by to see her tomorrow or something. She made me promise to call her. She wanted to have the baby talk with me but as usual, Mack was ruining things.

17.

LAILA

I'm sitting at the house wondering where Reek went and if that was in fact his car I saw parked out front of the restaurant earlier. I shook it off as paranoia. I had been a lot more paranoid than usual, lately. I mean, can you blame me? I was playing a dirty game with two of the most vicious men in Detroit. My leg bounced and I chewed on my bottom lip, as I sat on the couch unsure of what my next move would be. I've never been this nervous about anything. I knew what Vice would do to me if he found out the truth. And I didn't feel safe at all.

You don't know much about me and that's all Vice's fault. Because of him, I haven't really been in the spotlight. He kept me away from the life he lived. Little did he know, I knew all about the drug cartel he was in charge of. Obviously, I'm not who I've claimed to be. In fact, I'm the exact opposite. I'm a FBI agent working undercover to finally put his no good ass under the prison. But first I needed to get myself involved. I needed Vice to trust me but it was like the man didn't trust anybody with a pulse! I thought that after Olivia told him my write up came back squeaky clean, he'd let me in. All he did was take me on stupid sister-brother dates. I appreciated the time we spent together but I needed to be close to the drugs and murder.

I've even built a strong relationship with Storm. I just knew she was naïve enough to fold. I kept inquiring about Vice's profession and even she was telling me about some bogus ass gambling habit. I wanted to blurt out about how I knew about the drugs but then I'd blow my cover. I had to play it smooth. Especially since I was starting to have real feelings for Reek.

I've never felt for a man the way I feel for him. Actually, he's my first boyfriend since I left the boarding school. That man Vice saw beating on me was a stranger. Some man I lured into whooping my ass. Like I said, I learned a lot about him before I was given this assignment. And I knew he despised everything about domestic violence. When our informant, Dawson, told us where he was heading I hurried to the gas station. I purposely got my ass beat just so he would stop and help. It was risky, but being an agent was risky period.

Anyway, courting Reek was a part of the plan from the get-go. I was supposed to get him to confess his love to me and then talk about how he needed to leave the drug game for me. And then that's when I'd get info about Vice's drug ring. But things didn't work out that way for me. I ended up catching feelings. The FBI realized that and forbad me to see him. But I couldn't help it. I had fallen in love. All of the things I did for him to show my love and Reek still haven't told me a damn thing. Even he was talking about being a damn gambler! The people Vice has in his corner are loyal as hell, I can definitely say that. I didn't even come off as suspicious and they still didn't let me in!

Once I realized they weren't going to break, I played on Vice's emotions. There were nights when I would spend the night at he and Storms house. I'd pretend to cry in the bathroom, or some time's I'd just be depressed. And every time he asked what was wrong, I'd mention the molestation. I knew he was a stone cold killer who didn't tolerate betrayal so I was trying to get him to commit murder. I knew I'd need evidence which is why I gave a special 'favorite brother' keychain that unbeknownst to him, was actually a camera. Every day, I downloaded the files onto my computer.

My phone rang and it was Officer Olivia Thompson.

I answered, "Yes?"

"Vince Williams was found in his home, murdered."

"Great! That means we got 'em now. I'm about to pull the file up now."

"Great work, Bianca." Said Olivia before we hung up.

231

During my little introduction, I forgot to mention how my name isn't Laila. I'm Bianca Woods and I attended boarding school with Laila – Vice's actual sister. Once the FBI got whiff of me previously attending school with the infamous Vice's, sister they snatched me right out of the academy. It helped that she and I were great friends. Helped even more that I was of the same complexion of Laila. Only difference was...I took my eye contacts out and rubbed my irritated eyes. I was born with dark brown eyes, not light. Vice took one look at me and thought I was his estranged sister. But she died three years ago.

18.

VICE

Bitch must've been out of her fucking mind to try to cross me. Fuck wrong with this bitch? Anybody with sense would know not to go against God. I'm sure she knew all about me. She heard the horror stories and still wanted to fuck around with me? I didn't give a fuck and that was obvious. As soon as bro put the evidence in my face whatever love I had for her went out of the window. I knew I couldn't trust a soul out to this bitch. I just thought me and Lay was better than that. I was blinded by the past though. Thrown off by who she use to be. When Olivia told me Laila was straight I went straight into brother mode. Looked out for the disloyal, snake, pig ass bitch on some one hundred shit. Why is it that damn near everybody I show love to, shit on me in the end? But peep though, where them pussy niggas at? Dead and gone just like this fed ass bitch is about to be.

"Call her." I told Reek as I sat at the table with my shoulders slouched over, mug on my face.

He nodded and dialed her up. I was more pissed at the fact that I killed for the bitch. I promised to send our pops to his maker and I did just that. My mood been off since I did it. And usually, I never feel like this after I take a nigga out. At first I thought it was because I killed my pops. Now I know exactly what it was. I was shedding blood, ripping the life out of a man for a worthless ass bitch who didn't deserve vengeance.

I found out where he was staying a couple of weeks ago. I hadn't seen him in over fifteen years so I stood outside of his crib, heart racing second guessing what the fuck I was about to do. Of course the nigga deserved to die because of what he did but something was keeping me grounded like my feet were stuffed in concrete.

When I walked in, he was sitting in a recliner, in front of the TV. He was sipping from a can of beer, posted. He didn't even turn around to acknowledge me. It was like he knew I was coming. What came out of his mouth next shook a nigga.

"I was waiting on you to show up."

I touched the back of his head with the barrel of my gun and said, "What nigga?"

"You can't respect me enough to face me?" he asked, clearly unfazed although he knew death was near.

I kept the pistol up as I slowly maneuvered around the big chair. And I was eye-to-eye with what I didn't want to face. I'm a splitting image of my old man. Staring at him was like staring in the mirror. We were damn near identical except for the obvious age he had on him. It was like pulling the burner on myself.

"How you been, son?" he asked, staring me in the eyes with the same hazel eyes I owned.

I bit down on my bottom lip and put the burner in his face, "Stop talking."

He chuckled, "You don' let that girl get in your head too huh? She's sick."

I cocked the gun back and yelled, "Nigga, I said stop talking."

"I knew she was going to poison your mind us soon as I seen y'all together."

"Fuck you mean? Nigga you ain't seen me since before mom's passed away."

"I've watched you every day since I left. Your momma didn't want me around you because of the lies Lay told."

I touched his forehead with the gun, "Of course you denying it. What kind of sick fuck wanna own up to that shit."

He looked down at the newspaper in his lap and said, "January 12th. My death date. I would've never known." And then he looked up at me, "I never wanted this life for you, Vice. This monster you turned to...I wanted more for you."

"Fuck you, Vince," I said before pulling the trigger.

His head jerked back from the impact of the bullet. I stood there looking down at him. I had to get the shit over with. The more I stood there, the more I second guessed what I was doing. I thought I would've felt a little better after murking him but I felt worse. I took one last look at him before I left.

"She on her way."

"How she sound?"

"Pissed and confused, bro." said Reek laughing before he sipped from his bottle of red Faygo pop.

I nodded and pulled my phone from my pocket and scrolled down to her number. Like a bitch hungry for the dick, she picked up.

"Hey."

"My dick needs some attention. Come put your mouth on it."

I knew Olivia was about to jump on the opportunity to fuck with me. I haven't done anything else with her since the first time. I wasn't lying when I said I wasn't fucking with the bitch since Storm and I were back together. Since she made sure I wasn't mentioned in the involvement of the shootout between Tech and I she's been on my head heavy about fucking again. I kept hitting her off with excuses, though.

She purred and said, "Where are you?"

I gave her the address and hung up on her. I sat there with my fingers intertwined, pissed. I couldn't wait to put hot lead in both of these bitch's heads. How the fuck they think they could get one over on me? They might think they have a nigga but... nah never. I meant it when I said I was untouchable. I'll never step foot in a prison. I might've been thrown off a little but I'm always on my P's and Q's. Believe me when I say, shit is smooth. I just have to get rid of these ho's. One more loose end left to tie up. I had already given Reek the hood's. I ended up telling him about Storm's pregnancy, obviously. I had to. I wanted out of the game and the only nigga legit enough to pass 'em down to was Reek. My right mothafuckin hand. The realest nigga I fucked with out here.

Ten minutes later, Laila knocked on the door. I moved out of eyesight so bro could open up without her seeing me. If she would've peeped me, mean mugging, she would've ran way. I didn't need that. I didn't have time to be chasing bitches around the city.

He let her in and wrapped his arms around her and kissed her on the lips. If we were under different circumstances, that would've rubbed me wrong. Now I didn't give a fuck about whatever relationship they had going on behind my back. Fuck Laila. Shiesty ass bitch. I don't even consider her my sister anymore. Didn't give a got damn about her. Just like I stopped caring about Dawson once I found out he was a snake.

"What's going on baby? Why are we meeting at a hotel?" Laila asked as Reek was closing the door.

"Because bitch, I needed to get you here. Didn't want to ruin the carpet in the sweet ass crib I copped for you. I plan on flipping it, seeing as though, you won't have use for it anymore." I said, startling her, as I stood up from the chair I was sitting in.

She flinched and turned away, heading for the door but Reek blocked her path.

I headed her way, with a menacing frown on my face. Nothing could save her from the killing I was about to put on her.

Knock. Knock. Knock.

"Viiiicceee, its meee." Sang Olivia.

"Do—

Before Laila could get anymore words out of her mouth, Reek had his hand clamped over it, dragging her to the back of the room while she kicked and tried to get away.

I snatched the door open and Olivia opened her trench coat, swaying left and right, exposing her nude body. I smiled mischievously and roughly pulled her inside. She thought I was on some rough sex shit. Especially when I ripped her coat off of her. But when she turned around, her face turned flushed.

"What—what's going on?" she yelled.

I tossed her coat on the floor and said, "Bitch, you know exactly what this is."

And then, just as I expected, she wiped that surprised look right off of her face. She even smirked and placed her hands on her hips.

"Well, honey, it's too late. Ain't that right, Bianca?" said Olivia, looking over at Laila.

"Fuck is Bianca?" I asked, confused.

Reek let go of Laila and she looked to the floor. I yelled, repeating my question and she flinched.

239

"Tell him, Bianca. Tell him the truth. None of it matters anymore. You forwarded the video, right?"

Laila looked up at Olivia with tears falling from her eyes, shaking her head. "No, Olivia, I didn't."

"What," she shrieked.

Finally, I spoke up, "You talking about that video she recorded on that weak ass keychain she gave me?" I smirked, "Yeah bitch, I got rid of it. Wiped her laptop clean. I put the pieces to the puzzle way before I even got you simple bitches here."

Like I said:... I stay on my P's and Q's. I told you to trust me when I said I wasn't stepping foot in prison. As soon as I figured out what was going on, we hurried back to Laila's crib. We ransacked the house until we found the computer. I cleaned every folder and backed up drive she had on it before I broke it in half and threw it out.

"Now, who the fuck is Bianca?

Olivia kept calling Laila, Bianca and she wasn't correcting her.

"I'm Bianca," said Laila. "I'm...I'm not your sister, Vice. Your sister committed suicide three years ago."

"Bitch...bitch you's a mothafucking lie."

I said, in shock. Never in my life have I ever been caught so off guard. This shit here topped every betrayal I've ever gone through.

She nodded, "It's true Vice. I'm a FBI agent. I was hired to make you think I was her. Everything – from the first time you laid eyes on me – was a lie." She moved her finger in her eye and looked up at me. One of her eyes were dark brown and the other was light.

I pulled my gun from my waistband and aimed it at her. She cried, "If… if you kill me they'll know. They know where I'm at."

"Lies. I read the memos bitch. You were supposed to leave him alone weeks ago."

"But the department know I'm here, Vice." Said Olivia, picking her coat up from the floor.

I turned around and blew her head off. Lies. No one knew. This 'affair' was a secret. I turned my attention back to Lay… shit, I mean Bianca and she was on her knees pleading for her life. And then, like a lightbulb, something went off in my head.

"Was what you said about my pops true?"

"Yes. It was all true. Your sister told me he molested her. Listen, I apologize okay? Please just let me go. I was only doing my job."

I realized what was going on. And honestly, I didn't want to waste any more time on it. I just wanted this shit to be over and done with. I didn't even have to ask questions I already knew the answer to.

I walked over to Bianca who was holding her hands up. But before I could pull the trigger, Reek did.

Eight months later…

19.

STORM

"Waaaa…waaa!"

"Okay, Star, I'm coming baby." I said as I sluggishly climbed out of bed to get Star from her crib.

Eight months had passed and I gave birth to a healthy cute baby girl named Star. She kept me busy! Breastfeeding is not a joke. I was thinking about sleeping in her nursery at night, especially now since Vice is in Vegas, partying with Reek for his birthday. I missed him so much and he's only been gone for two days. I just couldn't stand sleeping alone. More than that, I couldn't stand having to walk to the other room just to feed her every two hours. She literally stayed on my breast every two hours like clockwork.

I had Star Jameese Williams a month ago on September 1st at Beaumont Hospital. She weighed 7lbs 4oz. Star is a splitting image of me, except for the hazel brown eyes she inherited from her father. Life was finally complete for us. I've never been this happy and drama free while being with Vice. He kept his word and left

243

hustling alone. We have a nice amount of money saved up. And planned on getting married next month. Yes, girl! He proposed to me after telling me all of the crazy shit that went on. Even after confessing about fucking Detective Thompson, I was still willing to be his wife. I knew his reasoning behind it and technically he didn't cheat.

My momma is so happy for me and has even built a relationship with Vice. Mack was no longer in my life. He eventually came around and accepted the fact that I was pregnant. When I told him I didn't want him in Star's life when she was born he went into a fit of rage. I tried to explain my reasoning behind it but he wasn't trying to hear it. I cut all ties with him once he threatened to kill Vice for the thousandth time. Why would I associate with a psychopath who threatened to kill my fiancé just because I wasn't comfortable with him being around my daughter as soon as she was born? I didn't need that type of drama in my life anymore. He didn't even know where we stayed. I didn't tell him at least, but I'm sure Mack has his way of finding things out. Although he was very upset with me, I sent him a picture of Star and he in return told me congratulations, calling her beautiful.

I picked her up from her crib, and sat in the rocking chair facing the window. It was dark out, but our backyard looked beautiful, illuminated with the decorative lights I had the landscape designer place. I put Star to my breast and she hungrily suckled. My phone's notification went off and I pulled it from the pocket of Vice's hoodie I had been sleeping in since he left.

Carla (11:12PM): Hey sweetie, wyd? I know my god baby has you up. LOL. I'm coming over tomorrow

Carla's Star's god mother and now my best friend. No one will ever be able to fill Jai's shoes but Carla is a really great friend.

Me (11:13PM): Girl yes. Her greedy butt up eating. OK just text when you oyw.

I sat Star up to burp and gently pat her on the back.

She let out a soft burp and I said, "Ohh, pig—

BLAH!

20.

VICE

I grabbed the red and white roses, adorned by baby breathes and hopped out of the car. Brown skin was about to flip. I wasn't supposed to come home until tomorrow morning. And now, I'm surprising her with the same roses I gave to her for on our first date. I missed the fuck up out her. I had mad fun in Vegas with my bro but my mind stayed on Storm and Star. I couldn't wait to get back home to my family. A nigga was complete. Happy as fuck. Even with bad ass strippers in my face, I walked away and told Reek I was going home early. He didn't give a fuck. The nigga was living life. Fucking with high paid prostitutes, drinking the best liq, smoking the best bud. He was lit. Business was booming for bro and I couldn't have been happier for him. I was just happy not to be a part of it anymore.

I crept inside the house and followed the crying of my baby girl. I heard Storm shushing her before I walked in. I sat the roses on the end table and pushed the door to the nursery open.

"Brown skin, baby...

I stopped midsentence as I watched Mack rocking my baby back and forth with tears rolling down his cheeks. My eyes darted to the rocking chair and I took off running towards her lifeless body. My soul. My fucking heartbeat. My fiancé. The woman of my dreams. She was...she was dead. Sitting in the rocking chair in my hoodie, with a hole in the back of her head that was slumped over. I fell to my knees and lifted her head up. The bullet must've been lodged somewhere in her brain because her face was still as beautiful as ever.

"Storm... please. Baby...don't leave me out here brown skin. Please baby. Pl—ple...please Star needs her ma. And most of all baby I need you. I need you so much."

I was talking to her like she wasn't already dead, but she was gone and there was nothing I could do or say to get her back. I did everything right dawg. I stopped the shit I was on. I was living life on a narrow path. As much as I missed the thug shit I used to be on, I didn't fuck off in these streets anymore. And that was because I had a wife and kid to look after. But look at this shit! Look at her! She's gone.

I let her go, and looked over to Mack who hadn't even acknowledged me. Fuck nigga hated me so much that he fucked around and mistook Storm for me. Lil mama was rocking my hoodie because she missed a nigga. I missed her sexy ass too...that's why I came home early. Never in a million years did I think I was going to come home to this.

I wiped the tears from my face, pulled the gat from my waistband and took Star away from him. Mack sat there, shoulders slumped over crying hysterical. He knew what the fuck was next and didn't even put up a fight. I laid my crying baby in her bouncer sitting on the living room floor and mobbed back to the nursery.

I stood in front of him, lifted his head with the burner and he looked up at me.

"I...I wanted you! No—

I stuffed the gun in his mouth midsentence and pulled the trigger. The thunderous gunshot startled Star and she cried. But I didn't care. All I gave a damn about was the pretty brown skin girl I fell in love with who was now dead. And because of me.

I let out a gut wrenching cry as I dropped the pistol on the floor and sluggishly walked over to Storm. My heart was literally hurting. Burning, and beating out of my chest. I sat on the floor in front of her body and pulled her down onto my lap. I've never cared for a person as much as I care for her. I can't live out here without her. I can't live without her. I can't do it. I need to be strong for our baby girl but who's going to be strong for me? I don't have anybody. All I had was Storm.

I pulled her body closer to my chest as I rocked back and forth. I didn't care about the brain matter getting on me. Her body was still warm and felt good as hell in my arms. I looked down into her brown eyes and searched for the captivity that was there before. But it was nothing. They were lifeless of course but I was just looking for something. I placed my hand over her eyelids and closed them. I laid her down on her back and lied beside her.

Eventually, Star's crying stopped. And I fell asleep, holding my lil' mama.

"Storm I've been calling you all morning. You must be knocked out to not here Star crying like thi—

I opened my eyes and Carla was standing over us holding Star, with her mouth wide open.

"Oh my God. Vice! Oh Lord."

By then, Storm's body was cold. I wiped my eyes which were damn near stuck together from the dried up tears. I looked over at Storm and kissed her on the lips. I wanted her so much. I just wanted her to kiss a nigga. All night, I kept trying to wrap her arms around me. I needed her to hold me. I needed her to tell me everything was going to be alright. What am I going to do without her?

249

"Vice…you have to…have to let go of her bro." said Carla with tears now pouring down her face.

I looked up at her and yelled, "Get the fuck up out of my crib, bitch and take that dead nigga over there with you."

I was hurt. I didn't want to let go. How in the fuck she gone come in my crib and tell me to let my wife go? I mean, we ain't married yet but shit, we will be next month. I'm not letting her go. Ever. Fuck is this stupid bitch rapping about.

"Okay. Look…" she lied a crying Star in her crib and walked over to me. I picked the gun up from the floor and aimed it at her.

"I said get the fuck out."

Carla back out of the room and left. I wasn't letting go of Storm. Not even to stop Star from crying.

Ten minutes later, my house was full of cops. I tried to fight each and every one of them off until my body couldn't take it anymore. I fell to the floor and screamed, "Brown skin! Please!"

I couldn't be without her. As much as I knew I had to let go. I couldn't. Even in death, we were drawn to each other. *Like a negative to a fucking positive.*

-THE END -

Join our mailing list to get a notification when Leo Sullivan Presents has another release!

Text LEOSULLIVAN to 22828 to join!

To submit a manuscript for our review, email us at leosullivanpresents@gmail.com

Coming Soon from Sullivan Productions!

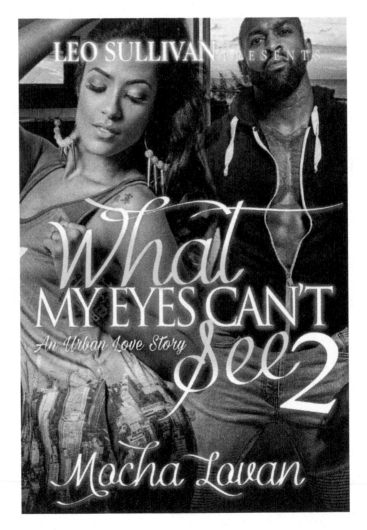

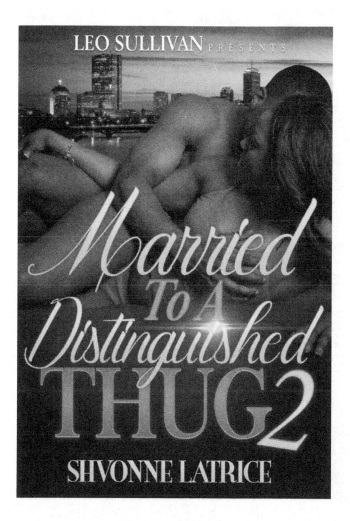

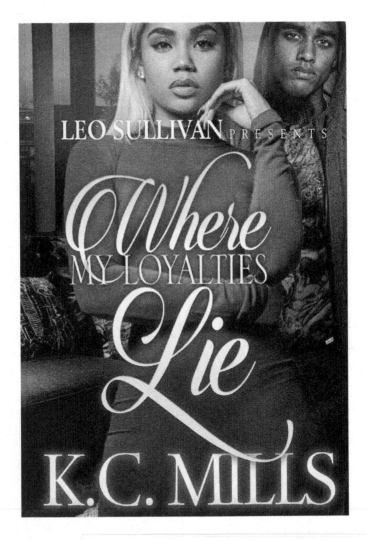

LEO SULLIVAN PRESENTS

Where
MY LOYALTIES
Lie

K.C. MILLS

US AGAINST EVERYBODY: A DETROIT LOVE TALE 3   MISS CANDICE

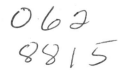

062
8815

CPSIA information can be obtained
at www.ICGtesting.com
Printed in the USA
LVOW04s1738021210

515533LV00009B/5/1/P

9 781522 807575